I0726185

JAGGER THE TEMPTATION

A WOLF SHIFTER FATED MATES PARANORMAL ROMANCE

BILLIONAIRE WOLVES SERIES
BOOK ONE

CHARMAINE LOUISE SHELTON

Jagger The Temptation: A Wolf Shifter Fated Mates Paranormal Romance
Copyright © 2022 by Charmaine Louise Shelton

All rights reserved. No part of this book may be reproduced or transmitted in any form or by any means, electronic or mechanical, including but not limited to photocopying, recording, or by any information storage and retrieval system without written permission from the author.

ISBN: 978-1-956804-22-5 (Hardcover)
ISBN: 978-1-956804-21-8 (Paperback)
ISBN: 978-1-956804-20-1 (eBook)
Published by CharmaineLouise New York, Inc.
Sexy Fantasies Fulfill Your Desires Publications

Jagger The Temptation: A Wolf Shifter Fated Mates Paranormal Romance is a work of fiction. Names, characters, businesses, places, events, and incidents are either the product of the author's imagination or used in a fictitious manner. Any resemblance to actual persons, living or dead, or actual events is purely coincidental.

CONTENTS

WANT FREE BOOKS?

Want to know what happened to Jagger's best friend Dylan? Find out in *Dylan The Rogue: A Wolf Shifter Fated Mates Paranormal Romance* **your FREE Book!**

Click Cover Below or visit **bit.ly/ CLBooksDylanTheRogue** to subscribe to my newsletter for latest news and launches, books from my author friends, and sizzling reads in book promotions. Plus, start reading the steamy fated mates romance for bad boy wolf shifter Dylan.

WANT FREE BOOKS?

FREE BOOK!

NEVER RELEASED!

EXCLUSIVE FOR SUBSCRIBERS!

ABOUT JAGGER THE TEMPTATION: A WOLF SHIFTER FATED MATES PARANORMAL ROMANCE

They say the heart knows, but what if it's impossible...

I'm the leader of my pack—the Billionaire Wolves of Miami. A wolf shifter who has it all—money, power, and she-wolves who vie for me to claim them. Sounds good? Not exactly. I long for my fated mate.

When my wolf senses detect her unique scent on another male, I lose it. Then memories forcefully blocked for ten years flood my mind. Memories of a young witch. And not just any witch—the future High Witch.

She's the one my wolf howls for, my fated mate. Now, I have to find her and prove it to her. Again. A second chance for us.

Too bad wolves and witches are not allowed to mate…

You've heard what they say about cats and dogs? Yeah, well, crank that up by a thousand percent for wolf shifters and witches.

No one is happy about this revelation. But that's too bad for them. My heart knows what it wants and that's her. Again.

Their steamy love story is a standalone in the sizzling Billionaire Wolves Series of interconnecting stories featuring wolf shifter fated mates romance. Get a glimpse of their dynamism in other books.

Anthem: "Never Tear Us Apart" INXS
https://www.youtube.com/watch?v=AIBv2GEnXlc

Visit CharmaineLouiseBooks.com

CHAPTER 1

 *agger*

"The quarterly numbers show an increase in profits. More than projected because of the opening of the beach-front resort in Charleston earlier than planned. The general manager reports the property sold out for the first four months…"

I nod as my Vice President of Hotels and Resorts for Larson Enterprises, Inc. continues his update. My mind focuses partially on his presentation.

For the last few weeks, I can't seem to focus. I don't know whether lack of sleep causes the lapse or something else. Dreams of another dominate my nights. They remain just out of reach, on the fringes. But it's their silent pleas for help that keep me tossing. A vibration from them of fear and sadness draws me closer. My instinct kicks in, and I want to save them, protect them.

Each dream brings me closer to them. But they remain just out of reach. I wake tangled in silk sheets. An arm extended as my hand reaches for them. Last night I called a name. However, as the last vestiges of the dream slipped away, the name dissolved with it.

I growl low in my chest in frustration.

My COO shifts his gaze to me. His wolf senses picked up my displeasure with ease.

I shake my head at Tag Dahl.

He cocks his head at me.

As my best friend, he's known me since we were pups. Born within a few weeks of each other—him to our pack's enforcer and me to our Alpha—Tag knows me as well as I know myself. I haven't mentioned my dreams to him, not that he'd think me nuts. No. I just don't know what they mean and if they warrant a conversation for analysis.

And Tag would delve into their meaning.

As my beta, he's my right-hand man. Anything that involves me and can impact our pack, he wants to solve the puzzle.

But this one will remain under wraps until I figure it out. So, I shake my head again and turn my attention back to the presentation. Even as I will my mind to pay full attention. I remove my personal hat. Then I firmly affix the one for my roles as CEO and Chairman of the Board of the luxury hotels, fine dining, clubs, and lounges company my family founded in Miami.

An hour later, a persistent Tag strides along with me to my suite of offices in The Larson Tower on Biscayne Bay. We pass through the executive floor as staff—wolf shifter and human—acknowledge us. The unaware humans often stare in awe at our formidable sizes. We're both six feet, seven inches of pure muscle and move with predatory grace. We nod in return but continue without pause.

I know Tag wants to find out what's up with me. I'll allow his henpecking since we're so close. Otherwise, I do not tolerate others in my business. No. One.

"Alpha, you have a few voicemails, sir."

"Thanks, Ginny," I respond to my administrative assistant as I open the double doors of my office. "Kindly hold my calls."

"What's up, Jagger?"

I bite back an irritated growl—lack of sleep will have you pissed, even at your best friend who only wants to help.

"You want a drink?" I ask as I unbutton the jacket of my bespoke three-piece Brioni suit and stride to the bar cart. It's after five-thirty, and I can use a stiff one before I head out to Club Sol & Mani for some much-needed sexual relief.

"Sure, thanks."

I take my time pouring two fingers of scotch into the Baccarat crystal tumblers. Absolutely no rush to have Tag pick at my psyche. My ears pick up his almost silent huff, and I chuckle to myself.

"Don't delay this conversation, Jag. You've been off for a few weeks now, and I've given you space," he says, then nods his thanks for the liquor. "What's up with you?"

Again, I allow him to question me, even though I'm his Alpha and my word is final.

I lower myself onto the dove gray tufted leather sofa in the seating area. Tag takes a chair opposite and places an ankle over a knee. I sip my drink as I consider my words. He knows better than to interrupt at this point.

"Dreams."

He cocks his head at the simple one-worded response. I shrug and take another sip.

"For the past few weeks, dreams invade my sleep. Every. Single. Night. Someone's in trouble. But I can't catch their name or where they are to help them," I sigh and stare out the window.

The panoramic view across Biscayne Bay with jet skiers and megayachts on its dazzling surface out to the azure Atlantic Ocean helps to quiet the inner turmoil my wolf and I sense. He turns his massive silvery white head to stare at me with accusatory ice blue eyes. It's as though he knows something I don't and pissed I'm not aware. I run my fingers through my white blond hair as I think on it, then shake my head. No clue.

"What do you recall?" Tag asks as he leans forward and places his elbows on his knees, the scotch tumbler balanced between his sizable hands.

I shrug.

"A brightness in the background prevents a clear view. I know it's outdoors since I hear the hum of insects and feel the warm sun on my skin. Naked skin. So, I must have shifted and returned to my human form."

Another sip of scotch, and I stand to pace my office.

Instinct tells me these are no ordinary dreams. But each morning I account for the whereabouts of my pack, and no one turns up missing. Not knowing who calls for my help drives me and my wolf mad.

I growl and toss back the rest of my scotch. A few long strides and I refill the tumbler.

"No one in our pack seems in trouble. I'll stop by the she-wolves' residences on my way home just to make sure. A few of our unmated males flew to New Orleans for the weekend. I'll shoot a text to them and make sure they didn't get into anything on Bourbon Street."

With a nod of agreement, I hold the decanter up. Tag declines a refill—ever the responsible one. Fine. It's not like wolf shifters can get drunk. Well, not too much. Our systems process substances differently from humans. All the better for us, especially when I'm in this pissy mood.

"Well, you know they say fated mates can have dreams about the other. The more frequent and intense they become, the closer the pair gets to their first encounter," Tag says. His emerald green eyes scan my face for a reaction. He knows I've waited all these years for my fated mate—and will continue to do so.

Despite my father's damn near daily persistence, I issue

the claiming bite and complete the mating bond with a single she-wolf. The last eleven years of nearly nonstop mating runs, with the she-wolves in my pack and those from nearby cities—hell, even overseas. Or galas at our hotels and mixers at our clubs, an accidental encounter, all to persuade me to select a she-wolf as my mate. None of them tempt me in the slightest.

All the she-wolves desire to bond with me. Then the supposed prince—and they were eager to lose their slippers and thongs for me to pick up——now the Alpha of the Miami Wolves Pack. Correction, *Billionaire Wolves of Miami* as the other packs refer to us. With good reason, since we're the most powerful pack in the South.

Several millennia ago, Scandinavian Viking wolf shifters sailed from the Old World and landed along the East Coast of what's now the United States. The six packs headed by best friends who sought new lands moved throughout the continent to form territories with ours settling here. We maintain close ties with our brethren through friendship, mating, and business. Plus, our Ruling Council gatherings keep us informed of happenings throughout the packs.

And even going that far and wide, I have yet to meet my fated mate. However, I will wait for her.

Hell, my wolf demands it as he gets agitated when he senses a she-wolf's burgeoning interest. Sure, he'll sit back while I fuck since it fills a need and doesn't equate to being mated. Wolf shifters—male and female—have strong sexual appetites. We don't have the same hang-ups as humans over casual sex, no sex before marriage, and whatever other bullshit they come up with. It's a part of our lives, just like eating or breathing. A need we won't suppress. Particularly with the built-up tension raging through my body. However, his pacing and snarls have increased recently, too.

So maybe Tag is on to something.

My *fated* mate.

A she-wolf whose scent I was born with teasing my nostrils. When she appears, I will recognize her by her distinct scent. No other will bear her uniqueness. Someday we will meet. I will give her my claiming bite, and we will have our mate bonding ceremony for all the clans to witness. I will make her mine forever.

The thought she may be in trouble makes my blood boil and my wolf snap his teeth, ears flat to his head. Our protective instinct on high alert.

So, I won't give up on finding my fated mate—or on us. No matter how many times my father bugs me about the need to bond with another. I'm no longer the teen who had to obey.

I am Alpha now.

"We're here, Alpha."

I glance up from my mobile screen and out the tinted window.

So focused on business emails, I didn't notice my driver

pull my Black Badge Rolls-Royce Cullinan into the driveway for Club Sol & Mani Miami. The flagship of six exclusive, luxury, members only BDSM clubs Larson Enterprises owns sits on Ocean Drive directly across from the Atlantic Ocean in a South Beach historic, beachfront gated mansion.

"Great, thank you, Cole," I respond. "I'll take it from here and will text when I'm ready to go home."

"Yes, Alpha. I'll get the door for you."

I wave him off and reach for the handle, only for the club's valet to open the door. A nod to Cole and a thanks in the form of a hundred to the young wolf shifter, and I stride to the scrolled wrought-iron and glass doors of the Spanish-style mansion. Laughter from members as they frolic in the mosaic-tiled pool within the sun-filled court-yard floats in the balmy evening air.

"Good evening, Alpha," the doorman says with a respectful bow of his head. I shake his hand and palm off another hundred. He thanks me as I move on.

"Hello, Alpha!" The two she-wolf greeters chorus cheerfully as I walk through the opulent lobby to the elevators. Another two C-notes and I'm on the elevator headed to my personal suite.

Tonight, I'll play in privacy rather than amongst other members in Exhibition where demonstrations and performance rooms provide entertainment—or inspiration. Nor will the Dungeon do, despite my affinity for the spacious section devoted to public forms of BDSM play. Those not in the lifestyle may think it's a medieval dungeon for torture with the St. Andrew's Crosses, spanking benches, chains suspended from the ceiling, and more. To me, the pieces and assorted whips, floggers, canes, and implements are only to be expected.

The soft thrum of sensual music greets me as I step out of the elevator and into the hallway. The rhythm vibrates through my core as intended to amp arousal for what lies behind the closed doors of the eight private suites. Members can reserve them in advance should they prefer the same privacy I wish for tonight.

Each suite decorated by theme has various BDSM pieces, implements, and toys. A nice variety of options to choose from. However, my suite remains for my personal use only.

I press my palm against the plate by the door of the corner suite, and the locks disengage.

"Good evening, Alpha."

My head jerks up. What the fuck?! I allow no one in my space without my consent. My ice blue eyes adjust to the candlelit room. On my custom-built mahogany wood, king-size bed cornered by four thick carved posters and a brass lattice canopy with rings strategically attached sits a she-wolf from my pack. And not just any she-wolf. The sable-haired hellion.

"Melissa, what the fuck are you doing in my suite?!" I snarl as I stalk towards her.

She jerks back as though slapped but recovers quickly. Fully naked, she rises from the bed with the prowess of a wolf in hunt mode and slinks towards me. Amber eyes glow in the candlelight. She tosses her waist-length sable brown hair over her shoulders. Her sleek figure with high perky tits tipped by puckered rosy nipples, flat belly, narrow waist, slim hips, and long, toned legs would make any male salivate.

Not me.

Even though I planned to fuck her tonight—after I *invited* her to my suite—my stomach churns at the thought as my wolf growls low in his broad chest. He's not happy, nor am I.

Melissa is one of my regular sexual partners. We scratch the itch for each other from time to time. However, it's not like we're exclusive. Many a she-wolf join me for carnal pleasures. As Melissa has with other males. And I've made it clear I am not interested in bonding with her.

But after this stunt, this may very well be the last time I hookup with her. If she thinks she can enter my domain uninvited, she's confused. And I will speak with the club manager about her gaining unapproved access.

I have no intention of giving Melissa any ideas.

Not happening.

For one, Melissa thinks she's the alpha since the other male wolf shifters in our pack bow down to her beauty and succumb to her whims. I won't have it.

Not to mention she's a bully. Another trait I will not tolerate. I treat everyone in our pack with respect. They may not be my equal, but I don't make them feel less than.

And the most important reason... She's not my fated

mate. The only wolf shifter who will enter my domain as she pleases.

My wolf agrees with a flick of his feathery tail.

"Melissa, I have told you we fuck. Nothing more"—I raise my hand to stop her response—"You have no right to enter my personal suite without my permission. None. Get dressed. I will inform the club manager not to allow you entry ever again. This is it. Do you understand?"

She blinks, then her mouth opens.

I fold my arms over my chest and stand with feet spread far apart in a dominant manner as I pin her with an arctic gaze.

Naturally, Melissa glares back and mimics my stance as her eyes blaze golden fire.

"Jag—"

"Alpha! Alpha, Melissa. And do not forget it. We may have fucked. But you will respect me as your Alpha. Get. Dressed. And. Go. Now."

She lifts her chin in defiance, then reconsiders when I slap my sizable palm on my muscular thigh. Her eyes widen at the warning. Then she scurries to the chair and gathers her clothes to her flushed chest.

"Yes, Alpha!" She exclaims.

With a stern eye, I watch as she dresses quickly.

Melissa stops at the door and glances at me over her shoulder. Her oval-shaped face pinched with worry. She knows she took it too far this time.

"Sorry, Alpha," she whispers, then opens the door and leaves.

I sigh and sink onto the bed.

Well, there goes the idea of releasing tension. More just built up.

With his tongue hanging out from the side of his mouth, my wolf yips. Ice blue eyes gleam with mirth. It's as though he laughs at my misfortune.

I growl at him and slump back on the navy blue silk pillows. My thoughts drift to my conversation with Tag. Perhaps fate doesn't want me with another since my mate will appear soon. My eyes close on a sigh.

Where are you?

age

"HELLO, darling. You came to my mind. How are you?"

Aaaw, so touching.

My heart should flutter as I swoon to the floor, so overcome by my loving fiancé's sweet concern. But it does not. At. All.

Fortunately, we're not on FaceTime, as Rupert Ravenheart prefers to communicate with me since he's miles away up in New York City and I'm in Miami. Otherwise, he'd notice the tortured expression on my face. And yes, the long-distance romance does very little to make my heart grow fonder for him.

Many females would consider me crazy to not fall at

Rupert's feet, so taken by his masculine beauty and magnetic personality.

I can admit he's model handsome. A flawless, clean-shaven sculpted face, shoulder-length, straight jet black hair with equally dark obsidian eyes that draw you into their depths. Six feet, six inches of sun-kissed skin cover his lean-muscled frame.

But…

Rupert does nothing for me. No desperate yearning when I gaze at him. Not a sizzle of erotic electricity when our fingers touch. No sense of loss when we're apart—miles or separated by rooms. What I've always expected of my mate. A passion that lingers on the fringes of my thoughts that arouses me when I let it wash over me in pleasurable waves. But with Rupert. N.O.T.H.I.N.G.

And I know why.

My mother Prudence Waters.

He's a part of *her* plan for *my* life. A plan created the moment she felt the spark in her womb when my parents conceived me. Just as her mother did with her at her conception. As the first-born females, our futures never vary from generation to generation in all our millennia.

We're immortal witches—the rarest of the rare—who stop aging at twenty-nine. Our line descends from witches who left Nubia—the land south of present-day Egypt and north of Sudan, and its civilization predates both—millennia ago. Their migration led them to this continent. Covens dispersed to various areas of what's now the United States, Canada, and Mexico. Some went even further to Central America into Latin America. My ancestors established our coven in the area of present-day Miami.

In our matriarchal society, it's the eldest daughter who replaces her mother as leader of their coven. And in my case, the additional roles of High Witch—since we're the most powerful coven of all, even beyond the continent—and the head of the Witch Council. It's expected of me to carry the mantle—rather, in our case, to wear the Waters Talisman—and stick with the plan.

Marry Rupert Ravenheart. In a week…

Aargh!

At my birth, my and his mothers betrothed us to bond the covens of the South and the Northeast—the second most powerful. Rupert is the eldest son of their coven's leader and five years older than me at thirty-three. For the last ten years, we've been officially engaged with a ring and a date. A date for my twenty-second birthday, then my twenty-fifth, and now my twenty-eighth.

Yes, each time I found an excuse to delay the intended nuptials. I wanted to graduate from Spelman College, then for them to coincide with a quarter of a century. Now, my mother put an end to me dragging my feet with the pronouncement of the wedding date with invitations sent to those worthy of attendance and a gown selected. Again, no input from me. At. All. I certainly wouldn't have chosen a pouf of a princess ballgown.

Not that I care since I dread the coming day, anyway. At the very thought of it, my head feels like a sledgehammer hit it and my stomach roils. I have to take a nap just to clear my mind. And it's only gotten worse as the day nears.

Aargh… Aargh!

I close my eyes and inhale deeply to clear my musings before I answer Rupert. My eyes open on the exhalation, and I paste a smile on my face. They say if you smile when you talk it perks up your voice. We'll see.

"Oh, how sweet of you, Rupert. I'm well, thank you."

"Wonderful, darling! It's always lovely to hear your voice. So, I'm glad I called…"

He rambles on, none the wiser of my false cheer.

"—saying, Sage? Darling, are you there?"

His questions draw me back to his conversation.

Quickly, I recover.

"Y—Yes, of course, Rupert! I have a vendor call in a few minutes. Do you mind if I ring off?"

Silence follows my question, and I squirm in my seat.

Does he notice I'm lying? I mean, he is a witch and has magick. I just don't know what—never bothered to ask, really.

"Not at all, darling," Rupert replies at last, then snaps his fingers. "Ah, yes, I just remembered! Enjoy your bachelorette party tonight. Do nothing naughty, darling."

I cringe as my eyes squeeze shut. Tightly.

Aargh!

The party slipped my mind, of course.

"I won't!" I squeak.

Another beat of silence, then Rupert asks, "Sage, are you sure you're okay?"

"Absolutely! But, listen, I have to go. Talk soon, Byeee!" I press the end button on my mobile and drop it on my drafting table. The heels of my palms cover my eyelids as I practice my deep breathing exercises.

"Sage, are you okay?"

I jump at the voice behind me and spin around on my stool. If it weren't a feminine tone, I would have thought Rupert used teleportation to get here in moments. Instead, I find my younger sisters—Willow and Lillie—in the doorway of my office above my Sage's Gems & Jewels luxury custom-made jewelry boutique in The Waters Tower Mall.

I wave my hands and shake my head.

"Yes, yes, I'm fine. A bit of a headache, that's all," I respond as I hop off the stool and hug the identical twins. "What brings you here?"

Willow and Lillie turn their heads towards the other, do some twin-mind communication, then swivel at me. Their narrowed emerald green eyes—so like mine, a maternal trait—scan my face.

I try my best to remain stoic. But I sense heat rising beneath my toffee-colored cheeks. With my extraordinary powers, I could fashion a glamour to disguise my flush. But magick doesn't work on family members and mates. The Twins would see right through the temporary guise. Then they'd really question me. And I don't need it right now.

"Hello? You didn't answer my question. Not that I mind you coming to see me. But what's up?" I ask to end their analysis.

They nod as grins spread across their beautiful faces, again so like mine.

Many people think we're triplets, even though they're four years younger. Add our mother to the group, and we're quadruplets. We're so similar, it's like peering into the mirror at our individual reflections. Our heights hint at who's who with The Twins five feet, four inches, me an inch taller, and our mother two more than me.

While my sisters and I vary the styles of our waist-length ebony curls, Prudence wears hers wound in a bun at the nape of her neck. Some would think it's severe, but the hairstyle serves to highlight her sculpted cheekbones and flawless toffee-colored skin. My mother is stunning and doesn't look a day older than twenty-nine despite being centuries old. No glamour needed.

"Party time, Ms. Bride-to-Be!" Lillie exclaims as she claps her hands.

Willow throws her hands in the air and wiggles her curvy hips. "Yes! We are going to have a blast tonight, Sage!"

"I can't believe you haven't pushed the wedding date back again. Mother was not playing with you this time!" Lillie giggles as her eyes shine and her dainty nose crinkles.

"Third time's the charm—no pun!" Willow adds, doubling over with laughter.

If only they knew the level of torment that besieges me. But I'm resigned to my fate.

Unconsciously, my hand touches the Waters Talisman.

The necklace imbued with magickal powers to protect

and to heal passes down from one High Witch to the next. It also serves to signify her roles and importance within our community. Over the millennia, some wearers re-set it. However, the original gems never change. Currently, the large turquoise stone with agate around it is set in white gold. The creator chose the gems based on their properties. Turquoise known as a sacred stone of power, luck, and protection. Agate to transform negative energy into positive and to enhance perception and analytical abilities. All qualities beneficial for a High Witch who must remain strong, clearheaded, and decide for all.

I wear the Waters Talisman with pride and dedication. In this instance, I seek its soothing and calming qualities.

My mobile chimes for the delivery of a text message, and I'm thankful for the interruption. As The Twins chatter on, I pick my mobile up from the drafting table. A genuine smile brightens my mood as my cousin and best friend's name appears on the screen—Anala Azar.

Hi! Just landed on my way to your penthouse duplex. Make sure the wards will allow my entry. Love ya! A.A.

Although Anala is a powerful elemental witch who controls fire and a badass vampire hunter, she prefers to fly on her private jet instead of teleportation. Don't ask…

"Who has you grinning? *Rupert?*"

And just like that, my stomach twists.

Aargh!

"THIS MUSIC IS PUMPING! I'm hitting the dance floor to shake my thing again," a tipsy Anala announces after she applies gloss to her pouty lips.

She, along with Willow, Lillie, and a few friends from our coven sip mojitos and cosmopolitans gathered around our VIP booth at the opening night for the exclusive Club Hati. My girls vowed to make my bachelorette party a fun night. I go along with the tasty drinks and pulse-pounding music.

My gaze roams around the opulent club full of the glitterati. Celebrities, socialites, fashionistas, and billionaire tycoons wear their sexiest, most revealing outfits. Bottles of top-shelf liquor and magnums of champagne sit atop the tables in booths like ours.

Partiers pack the dance floor with their booty shaking as they grind and gyrate to the DJ's booming tunes. Those not fortunate to have a booth stand two deep at the three bars or perch on stools at high-top tables surrounding the dance floor.

"Hold on," I shout over the music to Anala. "I'm coming with you!"

We weave through the crowd as the heady scent of various perfumes and colognes mixed with sweat assails our nostrils the closer we get to the dancers. I love it! The sensuous, undulating sea of bodies calls me to revel with them.

Anala and I make quite the sight as we dance in the middle of the crowd. Anala in a glittering fiery red sequin tank dress that skims the tops of the toned thighs of her five-eight-inch frame. Her ample bust nearly spilling over the top as she raises her arms overhead. She tosses her mane of ebony curly hair over her shoulder. Brown eyes dance with delight. She draws appreciative stares from the drop-dead gorgeous guys closing in on us as she seductively shimmies to the beat.

I match her moves with some of my own as I drop it low. The silver spangles of my fitted, strapless mini dress catch the LEDs like a spotlight. My shoulders shake as I rock back up to stand tall in my strappy sandals. Lost in the beat, I jump when brawny hands grip my hips to pull me against a massive chest. Trapped in the man's hands, I can only peer over my shoulder to see his face.

Golden amber eyes stare down at me from more than a foot above. Long silky caramel hair frames an angular face with a five o'clock shadow kissing the firm jaw. He smirks, and his eyes flash.

Well, damn.

"*Si, hermosa,* damn is correct," he rumbles in my ear. "You are a siren in your itty-bitty dress."

His warm breath sends goosebumps to the surface of my feverish skin slick with sweat from dancing for hours. The sensation of his thick dick grinding into my ass as his grip tightens on my hips nearly causes me to swoon. Whether it's the cocktails or the heat, I have the sudden desire for the man in whose embrace I shiver to have his way with me. Then I shake my head and pull away from him as my stomach clenches.

Will any man do? I wonder as he bows his head and makes his way through the crowd.

"Hey, are you all right?" Anala asks as she leans towards my ear. "He was hot as hell, Sage! You're not married yet, honey. You could've danced with him. Live a little!"

Her chocolate brown eyes sparkle with naughty intentions as she tracks his movements across the dance floor.

I follow her gaze and see him talking to three other big, beautiful boys. Their eyes shift to Anala and me. Grins that can only be called feral spread on their faces. They nod at us.

Anala wiggles her fingers.

I shiver.

"Anala, I'm not feeling too well. It's time for me to call it a night," I tell her as she half listens to me, too enthralled by the hotties. I take her arm and tug. "Come on. Let's go back to our table. Then I'm leaving."

I drag her from the dance floor and back to the VIP section. She giggles and follows along, swaying her hips in time to the music.

"Hey! We saw that guy grinding on you, Sage. Way to go, sis!" Willow says as Anala slips onto the white leather banquette.

Lillie frowns and asks, "Yeah! Why didn't you dance with him? He was smoking hot!"

I glance back towards where the guys stand. They still watch us and wave before I swing my head back around.

My girls laugh at me and call me a boring prude. They

remind me—as Anala did—my wedding isn't for another seven days and I should enjoy my freedom.

Sadly, I couldn't agree more. Yet, even the hunks—as gorgeous and tempting as they may be—don't do it for me. No more than Rupert.

Aargh!

Willow and Lillie drag me back to the dance floor just as I sit on the banquette. Their shenanigans and laughter prevent me from asking my driver to take me home pronto. Those thoughts fade away as more attractive—albeit drooling—guys pivot towards us. With a shrug, I let go and dance. The wedding is days away, and I will have fun now!

CHAPTER 3

agger

"Wow, I can't believe you actually came to the opening party, Jag. I figured you'd grump out as usual. Welcome back to the fun side of life, bro! Hey, maybe you'll even get laid!"

I growl at Viggo—my younger brother by two years at twenty-six—who winks an ice blue eye at me as I stalk past him to the floor-to-ceiling windows perched above Club Hati's dance floor. It teems with gyrating bodies. Scantily clad females, metrosexual males, macho types—wolf shifter and human—all vying for attention. And to get laid.

With a snort, I turn back to the interior of the club's office. Tag holds up a bottle of scotch, and I nod. I could use a stiff drink. My fingers run through my white blond hair and tug at my scalp.

Fuck!

The dreams have been incessant. Back-to-back every night this week. I can almost make out her face. Her, since the bright light lessened enough to show a petite, curvy female—although her face remains hidden in shadow. The urgency in her pleas for help drive my wolf and me mad!

"Here, looks like you need a drink."

I scowl at Tag as he hands a Lalique crystal snifter to me and chuckles. With a tilt of my chin in thanks, I stalk back to survey the club.

Viggo did a great job, as always. As the President of Clubs and Lounges for Larson Enterprises, Inc., this sits in his wheelhouse. My fun-loving and smart brother regularly increases profits for his division. So, he can get away with his dumb ass quips. To an extent.

I sip on my scotch as I watch the happenings below. The others—including Rust, my other best friend—sit around and shoot the shit. They're used to going out regularly. Except for Tag, who, like me, keeps a low profile most of the time.

I notice Enrique—one of our pack's deltas who runs messages between our allies and our enemies—cozying up to a stunningly beautiful female. Unfortunately for him, she thwarts his advances. I chuckle and take another sip of my scotch. Even though he's off duty, I have to follow up with him on a recent task.

Moments later, he enters the office in response to my text message.

"*Buenas noches*, Alpha," Enriques says. "You wanted to—"

A menacing growl thunders through the office as my wolf fights to spring free and launch himself at Enrique. My hands grab the sides of my head as the scent of my fated mate fills my nostrils. The scent of the Everglades after a spring rain woody and earthy with a hint of sea salt carried on the breeze from the Atlantic Ocean.

And the scent of *my* fated mate covers *Enrique*.

"What the fuck?!?!?!" I roar as I lunge at my shocked delta. Multiple hands grip my arms and waist. I fight them and advance, only to get pulled back. "Get the fuck off me!" I focus on Enrique and shout, "Where is she? Where the *fuck* is she?"

"Who, Alpha? Who do you mean?" He asks as Viggo swears while he, Tag, and Rust pin me to the floor.

I glare up at Enrique accusingly.

"Sage… Sage Waters! If you fucked my fated mate, I will rip your fucking throat out and eat your beating heart! Right out of your chest"

I LEFT my brother Viggo and my best friends—Tag, Dylan, and Rust—behind at the pack's camp in the Everglades so I could have time to myself. My wolf continues along a path in the Everglades at a jog. Then stops mid stride with a paw still up in the

air. He turns his head left and right, then tips it back to scent our surroundings.

I notice his pause in movement. But it's his whine followed by an excited yip before he tears ahead that rouses me. I push past the fog of self-pity and sniff. My heart races faster than my wolf.

My nostrils fill with the scent of the Everglades after a spring rain woody and earthy with a hint of sea salt carried on the breeze from the Atlantic Ocean. Sage! My fated mate is here! With another yip, I engage fully with my wolf.

We reach the same clearing as the first time we laid eyes on our fated mate. Sage faces us, having heard our arrival since we didn't bother to hide our approach through the trees. The corners of her mouth lift slightly as she watches us dash towards her. We stop, and I shift amidst crackling and a flash.

"Sage," I breathe, suddenly afraid she's a figment of my imagination. My eyes scan her face as my hands clasp her upper arms. She's solid, not a wispy illusion. Thank fuck!

"Why did you leave without a word?!" I ask, not bothering to hide my anger. "You could have at least said something. I've been going out of my damn mind. Do you know what happens to a male wolf shifter whose mate leaves him??? We go insane with grief!"

I rant on as Sage stands there held tightly in my grip. I won't let her go so easily.

"Are you all right? Did I hurt you?" I continue in the silence.

Her mouth opens, then closes as she blinks back tears.

Oh, great. Now I made her cry. Damn!

I pull her against me and rumble deep in my chest as one hand strokes from the top of her curly head to her round ass. An ass my palm itches to spank. Hard. How dare she run away from me—us?! It won't happen again. Or I will punish my fated mate. Soundly.

Sage winds her arms around my waist as she presses her forehead against my chiseled eight-pack abs. She's so tiny compared to my brawny frame. The perfect package.

"I didn't mean to upset you, mate—"

Her entire body tenses at the word mate. She loosens her hold on me and tries to step out of my arms.

Not happening. No.

I bend my knees to align our eyes. Her emerald greens filled with tears stare back at me woefully. Her lower lip quivers.

"Sage, you are my fated mate. Period. There is no denying us. Witch, wolf shifter, it does not matter," I tell her as I squeeze her hip bones. "How did you feel these past two weeks?"

Her eyes close as pain etches across her gorgeous face.

I squeeze her hip bones again, and she jumps.

"Open your eyes and look at me. Do not hide," I command.

Her eyes pop open as my mouth forms a perfect O in surprise at my tone of voice. Yes, I'm going all Alpha male on you, bad little fated mate, I muse.

"Tell me."

She takes a deep breath, then lets it out on a heavy sigh. But her eyes remain on mine.

"Not good. Not good at all. I ached for you," she starts, then lowers her voice. "I had more dreams."

I cock an eyebrow, and she tells me about them. I ponder their meaning for a moment. Then shake my head to clear it. Nothing matters except for my beautiful, fated mate being back in my arms. Where she belongs.

My fated mate awakens the most fierce side of my protective and possessive instincts. She's unfurled a carnal desire beyond anything I've ever felt before, deep in my soul. Mine! Only mine!

I pull her close and kiss the top of her head. Her unique scent fills my nostrils, and I sigh. Peace at last. Whatever we have to face, we will do it together.

My fated mate, my wolf, and me.

For now, I'm content to hold Sage Waters in my arms forever.

"Jagger Larson! Get away from that witch!"

"Sage Waters! Step back from that wolf shifter!"

My head snaps up as my wolf snarls and bares his teeth, ears flattened to his massive skull, ice blue eyes flash. A ferocious growl tears from my chest as I yank my fated mate behind me. My instinct to protect Sage heightened by the unexpected arrival of my father and, I guess, her mother. Their angry demands make my wolf claw to the surface, ready to fight for our fated mate.

"Mother!"

"I mean it, Sage. Step away from that beast, now!"

"Jag—"

"No!" I growl as I face down my father. Both pairs of ice blue eyes spark. "Sage is my fated mate! We will never part! Ever! I don't give a damn what either of you say!"

My father nods at Sage's mother.

She raises her hands as her lips move...

"Mother, no! Don't—"

Sage's words cut off as she crumbles to the ground, still as a stone statue.

My roar shakes the tops of the pine trees. I lunge for her mother. As I spring into the air, I loose my wolf, canines bared for the kill.

Her mother's emerald green eyes widen for a second, then narrow as her incantation focuses on me.

My wolf whines in mind-blowing pain, and we drop at her feet. The last thing I see is the face of my fated mate staring sightlessly towards me. An anguished cry forms in my mouth but never comes out.

As my memories flood into my brain—triggered by the scent of my fated mate—a formidable strength courses through me. I throw Viggo, Tag, and Rust off me and leap to my feet. I ignore their shouts as I race from the office. Like a mad male, I search the club for my fated mate, only stopping to scent the air. I catch a trace of it near the hall leading to the restrooms.

Mate!

I push past the patrons, paying no heed to their complaints. As I reach the door for the ladies' room, it opens. Chest heaving and wild-eyed, I stare into the gorgeous face of my fated mate, Sage Waters. With a feral growl of mate, I grab her arm and pull her towards the back exit.

Sage

. . .

"Now, I am going home. You guys can't kidnap me, you know—"

My sentence ends abruptly as the most beautiful male I've ever seen grabs my arm and pulls me down the corridor. So stunned, I can't react. My feet follow him as I hear Anala curse behind me. But he's too fast for her to catch up to us.

He slams a door. We burst into the night.

My senses return.

"Hey! Let me go!" I scream as I tug against his firm grip.

He's humongous. All muscle. Well over a foot taller than me, at least six, seven, I guess as I stare up the length of his broad back to his white blond head. He faces away from me. But somehow, I have an inkling I know him from somewhere.

He ignores my cries and tosses me over his shoulder with ease.

Startled, I take a moment to understand what just happened. Then I flail my legs and punch his back with my fists. Three cracks on my ass stun me still. What the hell?!?!?!

"Hey! Put me down, or you'll be sorry!" I scream. We're not supposed to use our powers in public. But being kidnapped proves an emergency situation. My fingers tingle as I invoke a spell to stop him cold. But damned if it doesn't work. I try again to no effect.

My mouth drops in shock at the failure of my powers.

Dumbfounded, I barely react when he places me on the passenger seat of a sports car and secures me with the seatbelt. The soft thump of the door closing breaks my fog.

I yank on the seatbelt as he slides in from the driver's side. Frantic to get free of the hulking male, my fingers react clumsily, and I fumble with the metal.

"Sage…"

I turn just as his nostrils flare as he inhales deeply. Then his mouth crashes on mine. Surprised, my lips part on a gasp. His tongue invades my mouth. It sweeps around as though tasting me, then tangles with my tongue.

My body sags as my brain short circuits. He literally kisses me senseless.

And I love it!

I lean into him, straining against the seatbelt.

He rips it free. Webbed cloth and metal tear like cotton in his sizable hands. He pulls me onto his lap. My knees straddle his hips, and the hem of my mini dress rises up my thighs.

I mewl as the thick bar of his dick presses against my lower lips even while his mouth plunders mine. As though my body has a mind of its own, I grind against him. My nipples pucker, and my core gushes to prepare for the beast hidden within his trousers. All thoughts of getting away from him melt under his wicked tongue and now his hands as they slide along my flanks and cup my heavy breasts.

His thumbs brush the distended tips. I arch my back and mewl into his mouth. He growls and nips my lips.

I cry out in carnal bliss. One hand leaves his silky hair

to snake between us. I must have him. Now! He growls again and shifts in the seat to give me better access. My fingertips brush the tip of his ginormous dick, and it grows even larger as it pulsates against my hand.

"Sage!!!"

I jump at the sound of Anala's voice.

The giant male growls savagely at the interruption. The vibration in his powerful chest runs through me. I mewl and cling to him, ignoring my cousin.

She bangs on the window.

I glance through the tinted glass, not sure I want her to rescue me.

The engine purrs to life, and the car leaps forward.

I bring my gaze back to—my captor?

He peers around me as he speeds the car down the alley and away from the club. His ice blue eyes flick up at me for a second.

I get dizzy under his possessive stare. My thighs tremble around his hips.

His hand pats my ass, and I gasp.

"We're going home now, Sage."

How the hell does he know my name? Better yet, what the hell does he mean by *going home?* Who's *home?!?!?!* I don't even know who the hell he is!

What's worse?

I don't even mind.

CHAPTER 4

 *agger*

I IGNORE the incessant vibrations from my mobile in the pocket of my trousers. Viggo, Tag, and Rust better back the fuck up and stay out of my business. I have to secure my fated mate at our home.

My eyes flick to Sage as she sits beside me in silence. Her gaze remains directed outside the window as I navigate my Bugatti Chiron along Ocean Drive, headed towards my bayfront mansion on Moon Island—my pack's private island in Biscayne Bay, South Beach.

I guess I should be thankful she hasn't demanded I pull over and let her out. Not that I would. I found my fated mate again, and I will never let her go. Denied Once. Never again.

Light from an overhead streetlamp glints on a diamond engagement ring.

A growl of possession rumbles in my chest. My fingers tighten around the leather steering wheel until my knuckles whiten. I burn to rip the damn ring off and toss it out the window as we speed along MacArthur Causeway. Then howl in triumph as the ring sinks beneath the inky black waters of the bay to disappear forever.

Just like the fucker who put it on her finger will once I get my hands—or paws—on him.

Sage jolts in her seat and swings her startled gaze to me. Her eyes search my face for the cause of the growl.

"Sorry, baby," I say as my hand slides from the steering wheel to the top of her thigh. At the touch of her warm, bare skin, my cock twitches confined within my trousers. I bite back a pained groan.

Sage nods and returns to the window. She doesn't shift under the weight of my palm. She lets it remain on her leg. I give it a pat and a squeeze.

Another win.

We continue the intimate connection until I turn off the causeway and pull up to the wrought-iron gates for the entrance to Moon Island. Two members of our security team sit in the guardhouse. Their eyes glow in the super-car's headlights. They recognize my car and wave.

Any other time, I'd lower my window and return the

gesture. But I don't want them to see my fated mate just yet. Despite me being Alpha, many in my pack will complain—or worse—their Luna is a witch and the High Witch, nonetheless. Too damn bad.

The gates' sensor detects its counterpart installed in my car, and they swing inward. I drive through and along the main road to my mansion.

Residences ranging from ranch style to two- and three-story line the road. Some front Biscayne Bay, while others have interior views. On the other end, in the interior of Moon Island, a mini town offers options for those who prefer not to leave our protected land. A school for younger members of the pack, restaurant, deli, pizza shop, beauty salon, and barber shop are available.

I glance over at my fated mate to gauge her reaction to her new home. Still quiet, she stares with no outward response. I'll take it as another win.

When we roll onto the driveway covered in stone pavers for my Spanish-style ten-thousand square foot mansion, my fated mate leans forward in her seat. The landscaping lighting scheme puts a golden glow on her toffee-colored face. Her emerald green eyes dance over the mansion's front lit by strategically placed decorative sconces and pot lights. Then shift to the water fountain in the center of the circular driveway. Her eyes widen at the large marble wolf on his haunches with his head tilted back for a howl. From his mouth, water jets to the sky. Lights enhance the beauty of the feature. Her curious eyes skitter to me, then back to the fountain.

I hop out of the car before she can say a word.

Sage takes my hand as I extend it to help her from the low supercar.

My nostrils flare at the scent of her arousal as her legs swing to place her feet on the stone pavers. She's so small, even in her fuck-me heels she only reaches my chest. My eyes close briefly on an inhalation. My cock weeps.

I keep her hand in mine as we walk to the front doors. They open when I place my other palm on the plaque. She enters ahead of me with her head held high, as though accustomed to coming home. The swish of her long, ebony curls draws my eyes to her round ass in that tiny excuse of a dress.

Who else besides Enrique held her close enough to feel her lush body? A possessive growl rumbles.

My fated mate tosses a glance at me over her shoulder as her heels click on the marble floor on her way to the opposite wall of accordion glass doors.

"Would you care for a drink, Sage?" I ask to distract her.

She shakes her head, never turning from the captivating sight of Biscayne Bay at night as lights from the surrounding islands and South Beach glow all around. Her curvy body silhouetted against the glass. I admire her view much more than the one outside for a moment, then turn to the bar. I need a drink.

My fingers run through my hair to adjust its wildness before I pour two fingers of scotch in a Baccarat crystal glass.

As I come up behind my fated mate—close enough to sniff—she turns her head towards me slightly.

"You're a wolf shifter."

She states it rather than asking for my answer.

"Yes."

Sage turns fully and takes the tumbler from my hand and tosses back the entire drink. I blink in surprise as she swipes her mouth with the back of her dainty hand.

"You said, 'mate.'"

"Yes."

"As in *me* being *your* mate?"

"Yes."

She nods her head at my empty tumbler. "Another."

I return her nod and stride towards the bar. My wolf senses detect she watches me intently. But she doesn't utter another word. As I stalk to my fated mate, her eyes glide over me from head to toe while her face remains expressionless. Back in front of her, she takes the drink and sips once before she turns to the view.

"You know my name. What is yours?"

"Jagger Larson."

"And this is Moon Island. Am I correct to assume you're the Alpha of the Miami Wolves Pack?"

"Yes."

She nods once and takes another sip, then cradles the tumbler to her breasts.

"How do you know my name and I'm clueless of yours?"

"Your mother wiped our memories with my father's permission."

At that, Sage pivots to face me. Her emerald green eyes wide with shock—and dare I say anger? They scan my face. I maintain an open expression so she can sense no guile in my words. She cloaks her emotions and takes another sip, then nods.

"When?"

"Ten years ago."

"Did you claim me before she… Before she did what she did to us?" She asks with a wave of her hand. I shudder at its similarity to her mother's actions so long ago.

"No."

She nods.

"But… I made you mine another way."

I place my hands—that have itched to touch her again since we entered our home—on her grip-worthy hips. My lips trace the side of her face as they seek the delicate shell of her ear.

"I made you mine when I took your virginity, *mate*."

She gasps and trembles in my arms.

"You are mine, Sage Waters. Then and now. I will claim you and make you mine forever."

Her emerald green eyes stare up at my ice blue ones.

"Well, we have two insurmountable problems. You're a wolf shifter, and I'm a witch," she says, then raises her left hand between us. "And I get married in seven days."

~

Sage

JAGGER'S EYES WIDEN, then narrow to glowing sapphire slits as they flick from my face to the engagement ring on the left hand I hold up.

During the ride, my head cleared. Well, as much as it could, considering his intoxicating masculine scent—a potent combination of pheromones, sweat, and yes, a primal wolf—allowed. I realized he must be a wolf shifter.

He emanates the sensual power and confidence of a lethal apex predator—a wolf shifter or a vampire. The feral growls—that send shivers along my spine and moisten my core—tipped the scales to the wolf shifter. The water fountain in front of his mansion confirmed my suspicions.

Despite our apparent sexual attraction to one another, a wolf shifter and a witch can never be mates. Not now, not ever. Especially since he's the Alpha of his pack and I'm the leader of my coven, High Witch, and head of the Witch Council. Talk about triple whammy...

All beings in the overall paranormal world know of one another. We'll even work together to achieve a common goal we can accomplish better together. It's not as if we live in our separate bubbles and don't interact. Hell, my bachelorette party was at a club with wolf shifters, and I danced with a few of them.

However, witches frown upon shifters of any kind. Some even refer to the wolf shifters as mangy dogs. The snobbish belief they're less than our kind since we predate them. Hence, the rivalry goes back millennia. It's ingrained in most of the elder witches.

Me, not so much. I don't despise shifters. Obviously, since I just wrapped my heated body around their sexy as sin Alpha. But I know I could never become involved with one. My future mate is Rupert Ravenheart. I sigh and shake my head.

"There's no getting around who we are. What that means for any chance of us being mates, Jagger. No matter what this attraction may be, you and I can never be—"

"NO!"

His roar rips through the air. The veins in his thick neck bulge as his anger punches the air. He clenches his fists and storms away from me to pace the floor of the living room.

I watch, unafraid. Deep in my heart, I know Jagger Larson would never hurt me. He's dealt with this longer than I have. Wait a minute!

"Obviously, you recovered your memories. So, if you knew we were mates, what took so long for you to find me? I mean, we're both in Miami. You know my name and who I am. It makes little sense," I say as the thought occurs to me.

Jagger turns to face me. He stalks over and towers over me. His sizable, calloused hand cups my face as he leans in and nuzzles my neck. He murmurs against my skin.

I shiver from his warm breath and soft lips. A mewl followed by his name escapes my slack mouth.

He rumbles deep in his chest—not so much a growl.

Rather, a sound that soothes as the vibrations roll through me.

"Your scent, baby. I lost it along with my memories until tonight. I do not know what happened. All I know is I scented you on one of my male wolves and nearly killed him for touching what is mine. The memories returned immediately at the recognition of my fated mate's unique scent. *Your* unique scent, mate."

I gasp, shocked Jagger thinks we're *fated* mates and not just a regular pair. To be the one linked to him through time forever?! This is a lot more dangerous. And impossible.

I back away from him, shaking my head.

He advances, ice blue eyes flash with a predatory gleam as they lock on my wide emerald green orbs. The rumble in his chest increases.

My butt hits the wall of glass behind me.

His forearms lift to bracket either side of my head. He leans down, soft lips hover over mine…

With the sound of his soothing rumble in my ears and the whisper of his lips on mine, I land on my bed. A strangled cry bursts from my lips. In the seconds it took for me to use my magick to teleport from Moon Island to my bedroom, the ache for the wolf shifter pulses between my thighs.

My magick works. It just doesn't work on him.

I roll to my side and cover my flushed face with my hands as a desperate moan slips past my trembling lips. Can we be mates after all? *Fated* mates???

Impossible for a witch and a wolf shifter!

No, we can never be.

And what the hell did my mother do to erase *my* memories *and* my scent? What caused the scent to return now but not the memories? Why did Jagger regain both, and I didn't?!

CHAPTER 5

agger

"Bro! What the fuck happened to you last night?!"

"You didn't answer your mobile *and* turned on the perimeter alarms around your mansion?"

"What the fuck, Jag?!!"

I ignore my brother and best friends now, just as I did last night—and this morning. My mind still reels from reconnecting with Sage and from her disappearance. Again! She pulled that same shit the last time when I was about to issue the claiming bite on her. Having a powerful witch as a fated mate may prove my undoing.

My hands ache to hold her against me again. To feel her

heat against my skin. Hear her soft moans of carnal pleasure.

Fuck!

I jump up from my desk chair and slam my fists into the pockets of my suit trousers. I spin to face the view of Biscayne Bay outside my office window. My sudden movement and back to the others silence them. Bunch of nags.

My eyes close as I visualize my gorgeous fated mate. How I burn to have her beneath me as I thrust my cock into her sopping wet pussy and my canines sink into her flesh. Her sweet taste lingers on my tongue from the kisses we shared. I want to plunge it into her spasming pussy and feast on her abundant juices.

Fuck!

My fists clench. I want to bang my forehead on the window in frustration.

I started to confront my father. Then decided it's best to wait until I have Sage back at my side. I want to make certain she's aware I will never let her go. I had to prove us to her before, and I'll do it again. Even if I have to give up all I own to make her mine.

"Alpha, a Sage Waters is down in the lobby asking to see you, sir."

A smile spreads across my face as I pivot and press the intercom to answer Ginny.

"Allow her up, thank you."

I stand and glare at the Three Stooges.

"Out!"

They squawk but leave. I follow them out as I slip my

suit jacket on and stride to the elevator. Ask and you shall receive.

The guys grumble as they disperse. Viggo and Tag to their offices while Rust—our pack's doctor and an emergency room doctor at the hospital—strides along with me.

"Listen, Jag, I'm not trying to get in your business"—he pauses when I cock an eyebrow and growl menacingly—"Whoa, bro! Let me finish."

"Fine," I respond with a nod. I value their opinions even if I choose to disregard them.

"Sage Waters is the High Witch. That's pretty taboo. Is she a tryst or more?" Rust asks as his hazel eyes scan my face. When I respond more, he runs his fingers through his shoulder-length dark ginger hair. A curse falls from his mouth. "Damn, Jagger. I'll support you whatever you decide. But that's a huge ask of the pack, bro. You sure you want to go there?"

"Absofuckinglutely!" I nod again as we stop in front of the elevators.

"Okay, bro, I'm with you and I know Viggo and Tag will feel the same way."

I slap him on the shoulder and smile.

The elevator dings its arrival, and the doors open.

My fated mate steps out. Her eyes find mine immediately. I notice a flicker of what I hope is desire before she glances at Rust and back at me.

"Jagger, I hope I didn't disturb your day," Sage says smoothly. I love the way my name rolls off her tongue. "Thank you for seeing me."

"Sage, you will never disturb me," I assure her. I place my hand on her waist and lean in to brush my lips across hers, unable to deny myself the pleasure of the intimate caress. She allows it but pulls away to glance back at Rust.

"Sage Waters, this is Dr. Rust Ingolf, our packs' doctor. Rust, this is Sage Waters, your Luna and my fated mate," I make the formal introductions with an emphasis on Luna.

Sage's eyes widen briefly before she regains control of her features. Rust blinks but extends his hand.

"Luna, I am honored to meet you, and to welcome you to the Miami Wolves Pack," he says with a respectful bow. "If you would be so kind as to excuse me, I must return to the ER."

Now Sage blinks but shakes his hand as she replies, "Of course, a pleasure to meet you, Dr. Ingolf."

Rust bows deeper, nods at me, and steps onto the elevator. As the doors close, the fucker winks at me with a smirk.

I bite back a snarl and place my hand on Sage's lower back to guide her to my office. My fated mate walks beside me with her head held high, regal, as though she recognizes she's the other half of the pack's Alpha.

The human staff don't pay any attention as my fated mate and I walk across the executive floor. However, the wolf shifters track our movements as they sense her level of comfort amongst them. I eye a few of them, and they have the common sense to lower their eyes.

Ginny jumps to her feet with wide eyes when she

notices our approach. Apparently, the grapevine reached her already.

"Mr. Larson, sir, should I hold your calls?" She asks as her eyes flick between Sage and me.

I nod, "Yes, Ginny, thank you. In fact, why don't you take your lunch early?"

She blinks, then nods. "Yes, Mr. Larson, as you wish, Alp—I mean, sir!"

Ginny scoots from behind her desk, grabs her handbag, and rushes away without a backwards glance.

Sage laughs under her breath.

"Please don't tell me I scared the poor she-wolf away, Jagger."

I push open my office doors as I shake my head.

"No, baby, she's overwhelmed to see her Luna so unexpectedly," I respond as I usher her through the double doors. "I'm glad you came. I was just thinking about you and how you disappeared on me. Again."

Sage turns and stares at me. I brace myself for her denial of being fated mates.

"I can't deny we're fated mates, Jagger."

My mind reels at her admission. But I keep a straight face and wait for her to continue.

"I used my magick to try and stop you from carting me away from the club. Twice. Each time my magick failed me. Keep in mind I am an advanced witch with unimaginable powers. Yet, they did not work on you," Sage says with an elegantly arched eyebrow. "Only a family member can rebuff a witch's magick… or their mate."

My heart soars through the roof! I want to pump the air with both fists as my wolf bounds about the office. But again, I hold back a response.

She continues.

"I have an appointment to speak with my mother in thirty minutes. I plan to question her about her involvement ten years ago. Since her actions involved you, I came to offer you the opportunity to accompany me."

Now, that's a surprising turn of events. Her choice of the word "confront" lets me know she doesn't plan to sit back and allow her mother to get away with what she did to us. To make us lose ten years together. For what? Because she's a witch and I'm a wolf shifter? Fuck that!

"Let's go," I respond, determined to move forward at all costs. I gesture towards the door beside a shelf where my private elevator waits and place my hand on Sage's lower back as she passes me. She glances over her shoulder at me and arches her eyebrow. But I apply more pressure to guide her forward. She doesn't step away from me.

The wins keep piling up in my favor.

As we wait for the elevator, I shoot a text message to my security detail to tell them to meet us in the garage. Once on the elevator, I admire my fated mate from behind my aviator sunglasses.

She stuns in a white suit with a pencil skirt that hugs her ass oh so right. I want to run my fingertips along her inner thighs up to cup it through the back slit. Beneath the one-button jacket a white silk demi-cup bra plays peekaboo. Damn. Her tits grew. My palms itch to mold to the D-cups as I suckle her tantalizing brown nipples. Hard.

Like my cock, as it punches the zipper of my trousers. I adjust its burgeoning length down my thigh. Soon I will bury my cock balls deep into my fated mate's sweet pussy and bathe her womb with my seed. Our one time so long ago will not be our last. The thought of her fucking fiancé going where I was first makes my blood boil.

Sage glances wide-eyed at me over her shoulder.

I stare back as though a vicious growl didn't slip between my clenched teeth.

She shakes her head at my denial and faces forward without a word.

The elevator doors ping open to the garage level. I place my palm on her lower back and guide her towards my Lamborghini Aventador J. Sage stops.

"What's wrong, baby?" I ask as I glance around us despite no sense of a threat—and it better not be on my territory. Karl, the head of my personal security and our pack enforcers, stands beside one of the two SUVs with the rest of my team inside. He glances around, ready to take out any threat. Seeing none, he nods at me. I turn to Sage.

She steps out of my reach and faces me.

"My car isn't on this level. I need to go to it, Jagger."

I shake my head and remove my sunglasses so she can see the seriousness in my eyes.

"Sage, when we are together, I drive. In fact, I will select four of my security members for your detail. They will rotate in pairs so you will have coverage at all times when you and I are apart. As the Alpha's fated mate and Luna to our pack, a good deal of my enemies may target you. I will protect you by any means."

Her mouth opens and closes before she responds.

"That won't be necessary"—she puts her hand up to stop me from speaking—"Jagger, understand clearly. We cannot act on being mates—"

"*Fated* mates, Sage," I cut in with a growl.

She sighs and shakes her head.

"That may be. But it's impossible, Jagger! *Please*! Let's just speak with my mother—" She stops and shakes her head again as she steps past me. "This was a mistake. I'll go alone—"

"The hell it is!"

I grab her arm and spin her on her sky-high strappy sandals. She wobbles, and I grip her hip with the other hand. I bend my knees so we're at eye level. She must have missed how serious my expression was a moment ago. She'll see it *clearly* now.

"Sage, it is not 'impossible!' You. Are. My. Fated. Mate. We will speak with your mother and my father to clear their bullshit up. Then I *will* issue the claiming bite, and we *will* have our mate bonding ceremony. Is that *clear*?"

She narrows her eyes, but I remember another chastisement.

"You used your teleportation magick to get away from me twice. Do. Not. Do. It. Again. We will communicate and not run away. Or I will put you over my knees and spank your bare ass."

She gasps at the punishment, then narrows her glittering emerald green eyes. I match her with flashing ice blue ones, giving her a glimpse of my displeased wolf. We glare at one another for what seems hours. Each refuses to back down. But I am Alpha, and she will obey me.

"You will do no such thing. Or *I* will find a way to cast a spell to make your dick shrivel up and fall off."

My fated mate issues her own threat.

I throw my head back and bark a laugh. Oh, she's not the sweet little Sage Waters of ten years ago. She's still a little thing compared to me, but feisty. My cock hardens to the point of pain, eager to make her mine again. With a smirk, I press my lips to her ear.

"That's not what you said ten years ago, *mate*."

A gasp bursts from her lips as her pupils dilate and a scarlet flush spreads across her toffee-colored cheeks.

I snicker and take her elbow, leading her to my supercar.

"Come, you've tarried long enough. Let us not keep my mother-by-bond waiting."

"I am telling you, Jagger, when we speak to them, that's it—"

"Come along… *mate*."

Sage's grumbled curses as she follows make me laugh harder.

But the thought of what awaits us makes my wolf snarl.

CHAPTER 6

age

"WHAT'S THE ADDRESS?"

"If I were in my car like I should be, you would follow me and not need the address!"

Jagger throws his head back and barks out a laugh. Again. His stunt irritates the hell out of me. Some wolf shifter Me Tarzan, You Jane nonsense! Like I need *him* to protect *me*? I scoff and give him the Brickell address for The Waters Tower, then fold my arms under my breasts, staring straight ahead.

I feel the warm breath before his words wash over me.

"You're so feisty now, *mate*. I hope you're that worked up when I have you beneath me in our bed. Not that I minded your soft mewls as I drove my cock deep inside your virgin pussy ten years ago," Jagger murmurs in my ear, ending in a throaty groan.

My entire body quivers as my core drips arousal onto the gusset of my silk G-string. My eyes flutter closed as I press my thighs together to ease the ache my fingers failed to satisfy last night. Or this morning. Damn this wolf shifter!

He laughs huskily as the supercar's engine purrs to life. He weaves the shiny red-hot number through traffic with ease. At stop lights, people gawk at the Lamborghini sans roof, windshield, and windows. Just two seats in this beauty. Jagger takes no notice of them. His eyes fixate on me. I ignore him.

We pull up to The Waters Tower's residential side. His security details stop behind us. The burly wolf shifters gather around the supercar. One opens Jagger's door.

The valet's jaw drops as he rushes to open my door. He barely greets me as I take his proffered arm. He hops back when Jagger rounds the front of the supercar with a growly, "I've got her. My men have the car."

If this is how he'll behave with me as his—

I cut that thought short. I cannot allow myself to think in that way. We cannot move forward with being mates. Period. A shake of my head clears it.

Jagger places his palm on my lower back as he glances around us. He needn't worry about any threat here. My wards protect The Waters Tower from humans and para-normals. He and his men will only gain entry since they're with me. Otherwise, the wards would repel them.

"Good afternoon, Ms. Waters."

I return the doorman's greeting as he eyes Jagger and the others surreptitiously.

The doorman, valet, and the rest of The Tower's residential staff are witches. The thoughts running through his mind question the wolf shifters' presence and Jagger's hand on me. It was bad enough hearing the wolf shifters' thoughts at Larson Enterprises when they saw me with their Alpha. This will only be the beginning, I think with a sigh. Then correct myself once again. Not the beginning or anything, Sage!

Jagger follows my lead to the private elevators for my family's residences on the seventy-fifth through eightieth floors—the penthouse levels. I nod at the coven members as we pass and ignore their thoughts.

Jagger must sense the tension rising in my body. He moves closer to me as his sizable hand strokes my back as we walk further into the lobby. Just for a moment, I allow myself to lean into his strength. He rumbles deep in his powerful chest. With each wave of vibrations, the tension lessens. I sigh, relieved once the elevator doors close.

"Although we're not mated—yet—I sense your unease, Sage. Our bond is stronger as fated mate than as a regular pair. You must recognize our connection. Do not deny us. We are stronger as one, and we will need to work together to overcome the challenges your coven and my pack will raise," Jagger says. The passion in his ice blue eyes burn into my very soul. He pays no heed to the two members of his security team. They don't flinch at his reference to me as his fated mate, just stand at the ready.

"Jagger, let's take it one step at a time. Please," I respond, even though my heart constricts. "There's so much to consider, so many involved beyond your pack and my coven. I'm engaged to the son of the second most powerful coven's leader. Due to marry in six days, remember?"

His eyes flash sapphire, and I see his wolf make his presence known—rather, his displeasure.

"You. Are. Mine!"

Before I can correct him, the elevator doors open to my parents' duplex penthouse on the top two floors, one above my duplex with my sisters' residences on the floors below. I shake my head and walk into the entry foyer.

Jagger's menacing growl makes my hand hover in front of the doorbell. I glance over my shoulder to see his handsome face twisted in anger. His men bear the same expression.

"Jagger, not—"

"My father is here."

My head swivels forward just as the double doors open. My mother and an unfamiliar male stand inside staring at us. He's a replica of Jagger from the imposing height to the white blond hair and ice blue eyes. Eyes that glare at his son.

"Jagger!"

"Father!"

They speak at once.

I glance between them, then face my mother. She stares

at me, expressionless. My lips purse as I bite back what I dare say would be a growl. I blink in surprise, then refocus and step forward.

"Mother, obviously, you know the reason for our meeting. So, let's not waste time. What do you think gives you the right to wipe our memories, and how did your magick work against me despite me being a member of your family?"

Her eyes narrow a fraction at my demanding tone and pointed questions.

I don't give a damn! She had no right to interfere and to such an extreme as to use magick against her own daughter. Unforgivable.

"Sage, watch your tone with your mother."

I look beyond her to find my father and another unexpected person. A woman who must be Jagger's mother sits with Wyatt Waters in the living room. My blood boils. They really came prepared. No matter. They're wrong, and we're right.

"Wyatt, no need. Sage is just overwrought. What with her wedding in a few days, it's understand—"

"There will be no wedding!!!" Jagger's thunderous declaration cuts my mother's words off, and the room falls silent. "Sage is *my* fated mate! Your magick kept us apart for ten years. No longer!"

"And do not think to try it again, Mother. I am High Witch now, and you will face punishment. Besides, I placed protection spells on Jagger and me. Ones I learned from the ancient grimoires. You will not break them," I add, as my fingers flex at my sides. I don't want to fight with my mother or anyone else. But I will protect Jagger and myself.

Prudence's eyes flick to my hands, a slight curve to the corners of her mouth.

"You do understand a witch and a wolf shifter will never bond as mates. Especially, as you remind me, you are the High Witch. The coven will not stand for it. Nor will Rupert's. You will not reject the son of the second most powerful coven's leader for a"—her emerald green eyes blaze as they flick towards Jagger and her lip curls in disgust—"*beast.*"

Chaos erupts as Jagger and his men snarl. His mother jumps to her feet—teeth bared—and his father growls.

I place my hand on Jagger's heaving chest. He glances down at me. His wolf contorts his face. Even without magick, my simple touch calms him as he takes a deep breath and relaxes. Then I face my mother.

"Enough with the insults, Mother. So beneath you, don't you think? Perhaps I need to remind you again. I am High Witch. Tread lightly. And that goes for you, too."

My gaze turns to Jagger's parents.

"You will no longer interfere, either. What Jagger and I decide is our choice. You took it away from us ten years ago. Never again."

Their beings shimmer, then fade.

*J*AGGER

. . .

"Wʜᴀᴛ ᴛʜᴇ ʜᴇʟʟ?!"

It's like my body dissolved, floated through a tunnel, then merged back together. My head swivels on my neck as I take in my surroundings. The view of Biscayne Bay. Tile floors. Oversized caramel-colored tufted leather sofa. My living room.

Next to the bar, Sage stands completely at ease as she pours healthy portions of scotch into two Old Fashion tumblers. She turns and struts towards me.

"You'll get used to it… I mean… the sensation will wear off," she says as she hands a glass to me. "I wanted to get us out of there and someplace… ah… safe."

Her cheeks flush, and she lowers her eyes.

I take the glass and grasp her chin between my thumb and index finger to raise her gaze back to mine. The calloused pad of my thumb brushes over her plump lower lip, tracing a pattern.

"Baby, I'm glad you consider our home 'safe,'" I croon as the rumble in my chest soothes her. "Here or in my arms. Where you belong."

She sighs and closes her eyes.

My palm moves up to cradle her soft cheek. She presses into my hand and places hers on my chest. My skin tingles beneath her touch. Instantly, I'm as calm as she.

We stand for a moment, savoring our connection.

"You were a badass back there, baby," I murmur. My lips skim the top of Sage's silky head and down to her other cheek. I angle her face to bring her lips to mine. I inhale her unique scent as our lips hover a hair's breadth apart. "You're right. The choice is ours and ours alone. And I choose you, Sage Waters. I can do nothing else. You are my fated mate, whether or not you like it. You know it."

Her soft breath teases my lips.

But I wait for her move as in my mind I command her to give in to me—to us—at last. The breath I held expels on a sigh as she turns her head aside and sidesteps me. I close my eyes and inhale deeply to pull my wolf back from claiming what he knows is his, despite her reluctance. I can control my beast. The question is how long do I want to.

I turn and watch her walk to the accordion glass doors as she did last night. This time, the sun glitters on the aqua blue waters of Biscayne Bay and forms a brightness around her body. She sips from the tumbler as she stares sightlessly through the glass. I wait.

"By the way, I sent your men to the SUVs," she says, then pauses for another sip. "Jagger, even though we're connected, you and I cannot move forward. A wolf shifter and a witch? An Alpha and the High Witch? No. Impossible."

My wolf growls and claws to break free. Sage—startled by the anger of my wolf—spins to face me. Her emerald green eyes widen as she watches me disrobe. I yank at the full Windsor knot of my silk tie and shrug out of my Tom Ford suit jacket. My fingers already shifting scrabble with the platinum cufflinks.

"Wh—What are you doing?" Sage asks, a tremor in her voice.

"Run… Going for a run."

My response emerges guttural as my shifts continues. I tear the custom shirt in two from my body. Sage's pupils dilate at the sight of my muscular pecs, chiseled eight-pack abs, and white blond trail disappearing into the waistband of my trousers. Yeah, what you're missing, baby. I snarl and toe off my A. Testoni Oxfords and Pantherella socks. Claws snatch open my fly, shedding the trousers and black silk boxer briefs. My thick cock slaps my abs, the bulbous tip at my belly button. Oh, so hard and ready to claim my fated mate. I throw my head back with a roar.

I allow my body to relax and accept my wolf to take over. My other half lives on the fringes of my being. Always ready to spring forth at my command, then retreat at my will. An ability born of our kind so long ago and marks us different from full humans.

The sensations of my bones reshaping and muscles lengthening to shift me from my human form to that of my great silvery white wolf block out all else. Crackling and a flash find me on all four massive paws within moments.

I swivel my enormous head to pin my ice blue eyes on my fated mate.

She stands transfixed. It's been ten years since she's seen me in wolf form. Her eyes scan me from snout to the tip of my feathery tail. Every inch of my body feels the intensity of her stare. Tingles ripple through me.

I ache to go to her. To rub my body on her. Scent her.

No!

My head shakes, and I pivot, bounding across the living room floor for the side door. My giant paw slams the button, and the hand-carved wooden door depicting a wolf opens. I race across my lawn, staying beneath the cover of palm tree fronds. My destination is the center of Moon Island.

Another perk of our private island provides a safe place for members of my pack to run in wolf form unencumbered. We run as a full pack in the Everglades a few times a month. The vast expanse and relative safety the subtropical wilderness offers makes an ideal setting for our numbers.

However, now, the island's oasis calls to me. I need to outrun the frustration my fated mate causes and the desire to claim her and to deal with the consequences—her ire, the witch hunt, my pack's disapproval—later.

I run past fragrant gardenia and jasmine bushes. Their floral scents fill my nose. But don't hide the unique scent of my fated mate. I might as well be in the Everglades after a spring rain whenever she's near. I snort and dash between some palm trees.

Glimpses of other pack members in wolf form appear amongst the foliage. Not wanting to be disturbed, I increase my speed and head towards the other end of Moon Island. I run for what seems hours. A normal wolf would have tired by then, muscles strained to capacity. As a wolf shifter, my body heals quickly unless silver is involved. Then it can be fatal.

Unfortunately, the pain in my heart doesn't abate as I

throw myself through the side door and shift. I grab a pair of black joggers from the antique armoire filled with post-shift clothes. Not that I mind being in the buff. Another distinction between shifters of any kind and humans nudity is natural.

I run my fingers through my wild hair as I stride down the hall towards the kitchen for a bottle of water. The woody earthy scent with a hint of sea salt carried on the breeze from the Atlantic Ocean fills my nostrils. Not just the lingering whiff of my fated mate's prior presence. No, the actual tantalizing fragrance emanating from her warm, lush body—

Fuck!

My cock hardens to the point of pain as pre-cum seeps from the swollen tip. I palm my junk with a groan. The thought of rubbing one out flits across my mind. But her scent draws me to the living room. I adjust my aching cock and follow her scent trail like a lovesick puppy instead of a fucking savage wolf.

I'm so screwed and not in the right way.

CHAPTER 7

age

A WARM TINGLING ripples over my skin. My nipples scrape against the white silk of my demi-cup bra as my chest rises on a deep inhalation. I close my eyes to steel myself for the male who drives me crazy with need.

The unsatisfied ache in my body blasts into me. I shudder from the impact as my core heats and moistens with my arousal. Oh, how I want to give in to Jagger Larson. My fated mate.

I close my eyes as I sense his presence closer. Near enough, the sexual tension crackles between us fed by pulses of erotic energy. Pulses that vibrate in my core. His all-male scent intensified by the sweat from his run envelops me.

"Sage, I expected you to have left."

He steps closer to loom over me as I lie on the caramel-colored tufted leather sofa. His ice blue eyes a deep sapphire drag over my body beneath a white cashmere oversized throw. He cocks an eyebrow at my suit jacket draped on the back of the sofa, then locks on my hidden breasts. A rumble rises from his chest.

My eyelids drop. But I catch myself and snap them open as I rise to a seated position. The throw slips from my shoulders. I catch it against my breasts.

Jagger lowers onto the large wooden coffee table. His thick, muscular thighs bracket my legs as he leans forward and wraps his fingers around my wrists. With a shake of his head, he pulls my hands away from my body.

"Never cover yourself from me, Sage. You are an exceptionally beautiful female, and I want to admire you always."

A shiver takes me as his rough voice licks at my skin. My mouth falls slack at his commanding compliment. Already peaked nipples bead tighter, and my breasts grow heavy under his hungry gaze.

"Jagger…"

His name comes out as a plea instead of the firm tone I intended to have with him when he returned. We need to talk. Seriously. Not dance this sensual tango.

I clear my dry throat and try again, more forcefully this time.

"Jagger."

The confident tone inspires me to continue despite his

heated gaze on my lips as he licks his own full mouth. A flash of a long canine shoots a thrill through me.

Aargh!

"Jagger, we must talk."

I almost waiver when his sizable hands stroke the tops of my thighs as his legs presses into them from either side. My eyes beg to stray to his sculpted chest and washboard abs. The white blond happy trail beckons to me to gaze lower. Lower to the magnificent bulge tenting his soft joggers. A damn flagpole stands tall. A pole I ache to climb and ride.

Sage Waters! I yell at myself to remain focused on the issues at hand. And there are many. Too many we may not be able to overcome.

Aargh… Aargh!!

His molten sapphires nearly crumble my resolve. But I persevere.

"This mating thing—"

His low growl makes me swallow and start anew.

"Us being mates—"

Another growl corrects me.

"Us being *fated* mates—"

He rumbles and smirks appreciatively.

"Goes beyond the two of us," I press on, ignoring the scowl on his handsome face. "Hear me out, please."

He nods begrudgingly, and I continue.

"We have responsibilities—you to your pack and me to my coven and all witches. Not just to lead, but for succession."

Jagger cocks an eyebrow, and I wonder how much of the male is present and not the wolf.

"You are the Alpha of the Miami Wolves Pack. You must mate and produce an heir. A male wolf shifter to carry on your family's legacy."

He gives me a slight nod. His hands still caress my thighs while his thighs press into them. I blink to ignore his erotic distraction.

"And as the High Witch, I must produce a witch daughter who will take my place and lead our coven and head the Witch Council."

He raises his eyebrows as if to say, right. I sigh because I must make him see how wrong for each other we are as mates—fated or otherwise.

The next part brings tears to my eyes. I glance away and take a deep breath. Jagger lets his hand move from my thigh to cup my chin and turn my gaze back to him. His eyes scan my face while my eyes flit everywhere but at him. He rumbles in his chest, and I sigh—this time in ease. I gather the courage to go on.

"You do not realize something very important about me, Jagger. I still don't have my memories. So, I don't know if we had this discussion before."

I pause and stare him straight in the eyes.

"I am an Immortal Witch. My twenty-ninth birthday is in five days. At that age, we stop aging. Forever. You saw my mother. She's hundreds of years old and gets mistaken for my sister every day."

My throat clogs with the tears causing me to pause. I close my eyes. A tear slips from the corner of one.

Jagger catches it with his thumb and leans over to brush his lips against my eyelids. I tremble beneath his soft touch.

"I know wolf shifters—all shifters—live much longer than humans. But I cannot imagine watching you getting old and—" My throat refuses to release the word, and I bow my head as the tears flow freely. They drop to my lap as I shudder.

Jagger moves from the coffee table and sits beside me, pulling me onto his lap. He buries his face in my hair as his arms band around me. I bury my face in his muscular chest and cry.

I cry for the thought of watching him age. For the messed-up fact we cannot be together. For my desire to be with him and hell, fuck it all! But I can't. We can't. A wellspring of tears flow from my eyes as I finally let it go.

Jagger holds me for an indeterminate amount of time. His rumbles help to soothe the ache in my heart. But not the passion burning in my core.

I want him. And I want him now.

JAGGER

I HOLD my fated mate as my mind absorbs all she's told me. The only thing that stands out is her desire to be my fated mate. The obstacles she keeps insisting upon do not matter. At. All.

Sure, we'll face opposition. But I give zero fucks. If my pack fights me on their Luna being a witch—the High Witch—then fuck them, too. I meant it when I said I will give it all up for my fated mate. The Fates would not pair us if we did not belong together. We may not see the reason now. But there must be one the Fates see we need to be together for.

The same goes for the witches. I couldn't care less. It's Sage's call with them, and I will support her in whatever she decides.

Our pups. Well, we'll cross that bridge when it happens. Hell, we may not have males or may not have females. We won't know until we try. And I damn sure am bursting to get on with that part of our mating. I want to see Sage's belly swell with my seed. Grow round with my pup inside her womb. My cock thumps in agreement.

But she's in her head too much with this whole situation. Not saying I'm irresponsible. Not at all. I know my responsibilities and take them seriously. But I will *not* allow them to supersede my relationship with my fated mate.

In an ideal world, the witches and my pack would accept Sage and me as fated mates. We would move forward and live as one in peace. But if it calls for more, my wolf and I will do what we must to protect our fated mate and our relationship.

I have to get her away. Give us time to be together with no outside influences. To reconnect. I hope being alone will help her regain her memories. Something may trigger them, like her scent on Enrique did for me.

A smile spreads across my face as I realize just the solution.

"Sage, I understand what you say, and I do not disagree. Except that I will sacrifice all for you—for us," I say as I sit back and cup her wobbly chin in my palm. "We need to spend time together, away from everyone and everything else. Reconnect. You and me. Come on my boat with me. Let me show you how good it will be between us. Five days. Just you and me, Sage."

She studies my face. I keep an open expression, so she sees no guile. In my mind, I chant for her to agree. After a moment, she nods.

"Okay, Jagger. I will go."

My heart leaps in my chest. I can't help the silly grin on my face as I pull her tight to my chest and bury my face in her silky curls. Her scent washes over me, and my wolf howls with passion.

I will persuade my fated mate nothing matters but us. Or turn the world upside down.

 agger

"OH, my goodness, Jagger! You said your boat, not a megayacht! It's incredible."

My fated mate's squeal of delight makes me grin.

After I told Tag to step in as my second to handle the pack and work while I take the next few days with Sage, I drove us in a golf cart to Moon Island's private marina. Karl and my security team followed. We walked along the dock to the tender where a crew member waited to ferry us to *Moonbeam*. It dwarfs the other boats members of the pack dock in slips. The 465-foot silver megayacht gleams in the afternoon sunlight. Five decks tiered from the back with a long front to accommodate a helipad.

Twenty cabins sleep up to thirty-six guests. For entertainment, it features a beach club with a garage for water sports toys, fitness center, spa and sauna, swimming pool and hot tub, media room, bowling alley, and a game room. Multiple living spaces include salons, wet bars, dining rooms, library, and an office with a conference room I can conduct business. I designed the megayacht with my pack in mind, wanting to provide the members with a luxurious water respite.

Now, *Moonbeam* will serve as our getaway.

The rest of the crew greets us on the lower deck as the tender nears the megayacht's stern. Lined up in their dress whites, the captain steps forward as the others stand at attention. He's a former naval officer who still loves the sea. Along with the others, he's a member of our pack.

"Alpha, it's been a while. So good to see you, sir," Captain says as the tender slips beside the much larger boat. While the bosun helps secure the tender, Captain reaches out to lift Sage to the deck. "Welcome aboard, ma'am!" He smiles.

"Thank you," she responds with a giggle as she smooths her suit jacket and pencil skirt.

"Good to see you too, Captain," I say as I step onto the boat and take my fated mate's hand. My wolf growled at his hands on her, even if polite. "This is Sage Waters. Sage, this is Captain."

He tips his hat and turns to introduce her to the rest of the crew. The Chief Stew holds a tray of mojitos. We take glasses with thanks. The chef tells us she prepared a late lunch of grilled Maine lobster and king prawns with cilantro lime butter and grilled vegetables and salted caramel pie for dessert.

I turn to Sage and ask, "Do you want a tour first or to eat lunch?"

She's already grinning, emerald green eyes sparkling with delight. "Absolutely lunch! I will never turn down a delicious meal. Thank you, Chef. We can tour after to burn off such a decadent dessert!"

With a smirk, I lean over and press my lips to the delicate shell of her ear. "I have a much better plan to 'burn off' calories, *mate*. Besides, I do not want you to lose one centimeter of your hot, curvy body."

She shivers. I place my hand on her lower belly and press her ass against my erection. The very same one I've sported since I found her still in our living room. I nip her lobe and step away. She gasps and sways. My hand grasps her waist and steadies her as a wicked chuckle makes her tremble.

With their wolf sense of hearing, the crew avert their eyes. The Captain hides his smile with the turn of his head as he instructs them to get ready to leave Biscayne Bay. I requested he charter our voyage to the Florida Keys. My fated mate and I will have plenty of time to ourselves and to enjoy the sights of the coast, then explore the Keys.

Before we return, I will claim her fully.

She bends over and removes her fuck-me heels, then holds them by the straps.

I band an arm around her waist as I lead her up to the

deck for outdoor dining. She wraps her arm around my waist and snuggles against me. A grin spreads across my face as she tucks into my side perfectly.

Another score.

How they do it, I don't know. But the Chief Stew and Stewardess beat us to the deck. They greet us with a mixture of fresh citrus fruits and melon for a refreshing appetizer salad. We exchange our empty mojito glasses for crisp and dry rosé wine. It pairs well with the starter and main dish.

Over lunch, our conversation flows comfortably. We don't discuss her concerns. Rather, I tell her about our destination and the fun to have on the megayacht—besides hours of making love, of course. It's as though ten years haven't passed. We're at ease with one another. As expected of fated mates.

My hope is Sage senses our connection is undeniable and worth fighting for.

After lunch, I take her on the tour. The megayacht impresses her as I knew it would. Once again, she's comfortable in the space. Walking about with ease. Until an hour later, when we arrive at the primary cabin.

"Oh, so where will you sleep?" She asks as her eyes flick from the king-size bed to me and back.

I chuckle and yank the collar of my t-shirt over my head. I toss the unwanted garment to a chair and stalk towards my fated mate. My blood heats with each step. Like the apex predator I am, her startled gasp and the sweet scents of fear and arousal mix to heighten my desire to take her without reservation however I choose. Now.

In a few strides, I stand before my fated mate and stare down into her wide emerald green eyes. Her swallow audible to my wolf senses. But her gaze doesn't waver. My hands reach out. Fingers make quick work of the single button on her suit jacket. I push it from her shoulders. It slides to the carpet.

Her brown beaded nipples stand out in bas-relief against the white silk of her demi-cup bra. I drop my head to suck one into my mouth through the fabric. She moans. Her fingers dip into my hair as mine slip around her hips to unzip her pencil skirt. It too slides to puddle at her bare feet.

While my mouth moves to the other plump nipple, I grab her hips. My fingers dig into the soft flesh as I anchor her in place. Thumbs trace the edges of her G-string along her mons. I tease her lower lips with a few flicks beneath the white silk. She mewls and grinds her slick pussy against my thumbs.

I growl and rip the scrap of silk from covering her pussy. The pinch of the fabric on her sensitive skin makes her cry out. I drop to my knees, throw her thigh over my shoulder, and plant my face at the treasure box between her thighs. My nose burrows between her wet folds, and I inhale. Deeply.

My mouth waters from her tantalizing scent.

Mine!

I lash my tongue in a zig-zag pattern across her slippery

seam, then angle her pelvis to reach along the perineum to her puckered hole. She hops on one foot as the tip of my tongue rims, then probes the forbidden spot. The gasp of my name rolls off her lips, straight to my engorged cock. Its head plus several inches pushes past the waistband of my joggers like a heat-seeking missile aimed for her cunt.

"Jagger! What are you do—"

Her question ends abruptly when my tongue spears into her dripping pussy as my thumb and index finger pinch her swollen clit. Her back bows as she wails. Juices gush into my eagerly waiting mouth as her first—of many I have planned—orgasm rocks through her. As her pussy walls ripple along my tongue, she falls forward, torso draped over my head.

The near suffocation is worth it to taste the sweet nectar of her climax. I gulp it down, already craving more. I add a finger to aid in my feast. It mines for more golden honey as the tip strokes the sensitive spot on her front wall. And as expected, her inner thighs squeeze my ears like a vise as another orgasm hits. I can barely hear her cries over the sounds of my munching.

I continue my delectable feast until my fated mate wobbles on her standing leg, despite me bracing her with my arm looped behind and around her thigh. Her hoarse voice begs for no more after many orgasms.

In one swift move, I rise to my feet with her a quivering mess over my shoulder. Two fingers dabble just inside her slick folds, enough to keep her on the edge as I stride towards the bed. The bed in which *both* of us will sleep. Later, that is.

I toss her onto the middle and salivate as her D-cup tits spill from the tops of her little silk bra. The plump nipples stare back at me, and I growl as I tear out of my joggers. Her hooded eyes linger on my cock as it bobs against my washboard abs. I fist the base and stroke upwards a few times. Her tongue moistens her lips.

"Oh, I'll fill that hole, too, mate."

Her gaze jumps to mine as her eyelids flutter. I smirk.

The mattress dips as I knee my way towards her. My smirk widens when her knees splay out to welcome my advance. I drop kisses from her ankle up her calf, behind the knee, all the way up to her slack mouth. I cover it with mine.

My tongue sweeps inside to tangle with hers. I swallow each of her moans possessively. She reaches for me. But I twine our fingers and lift our hands to either side of her head as I remain planked over her. When my fingers brush the engagement ring on her finger, I rip my mouth from hers with a growl.

"Mine!" I snarl as I sit back on my haunches with her left hand in mine and tug the offensive piece from her finger. I toss it to the floor, then pin her with my hardened gaze. "You will marry no one but me, Sage Waters. Me!"

She opens her mouth to speak, but I shake my head.

"Enough! You know the Fates plan for us to be together. I will not succumb to madness brought about by separation from my mate—from *you*! And damn sure not because you married another."

"Jagger, I agree."

～

Sage

His eyes pop at my admission.

"I cannot marry Rupert," I continue, then place my finger on Jagger's lips when he starts to speak. "But I am not ready to complete the bonding with you yet. Let's do as you said earlier and spend the next five days together, alone. You also said you would show me how good it will be between us."

I wrap my arms around his neck and pull him down to me. He's stiff in my arms, but I persevere.

"I'm here. With *you*. Now show me," I purr with my lips against his ear as I arch my back and secure his narrow hips between my welcoming thighs. My wet core throbs as it rubs against his thick cock, coating it with my arousal.

He groans and relaxes in my erotic embrace. Then he raises his head to stare into my eyes.

"One question."

When I nod, he continues in a gruff voice, "Have there been many others?"

Oh, my possessive fated mate...

"Only you, Jagger Larson. And I can't even remember

what happened. Make up for it," I say, then nip his lower lip as I undulate my hips. "Now."

His ice blue eyes flash deep sapphire. A glimpse of his wolf appears in their depths. Its hungry eyes devour me. Jagger blinks, and it's gone.

Is it crazy I want to see more of his feral other half? To feel the raw power it exudes as it takes me?

Jagger doesn't give me a moment to ponder the sanity of my questions. His hands grip my hips and lift them.

Balanced on my shoulders and the back of my head, I clutch at his forearms. My eyes dart from his face to his dick, that's even bigger than it was a moment ago. Long, thick, and veiny with a shiny bead of pre-cum on its deep purple tip poised at the entrance to my core.

"I can't be gentle with you now, mate. My wolf and I demand all from you, and we plan to take it."

Before I can express agreement, his hips drive forward, and he impales me on his ginormous cock. A strangled scream rips from my throat. He's so big. Too big. My fingernails dig into his forearms as my back bows. I'm torn between pushing him away and pulling him deeper.

Once again, he decides for me.

Jagger's firm ass flexes beneath my heels of my feet as he thrusts to the root of his cock.

My head twists from side to side as his bulbous tip brushes my cervix. And I thought he was inside of me fully before! A guttural groan escapes my mouth.

He leans over my body and captures my mouth with his for a demanding kiss. His tongue takes possession as it licks around, then prods my tongue. I have no choice but to tangle with him. I moan and give in. He growls in triumph.

My lower half registers his dick as it pulsates inside my core. The inner walls stretch to accommodate his massive girth and length. They match his carnal rhythm.

"This pussy is mine, mate. Only mine. Mine forever. You will never forget *this* memory of my cock claiming you."

His gruff voice filled with possessive-driven lust makes me mewl in response as my pussy clenches down hard on his cock.

"Fuck, yeah…" He groans in my ear. "So tight. So wet. You like how my giant cock claims every inch of your little pussy. *My* pussy."

"Oh, Fates…" I moan as my core spasms. The unexpected orgasm sends shock waves through my body, from my core and along my limbs to my fingers and toes. They dig deeper into his forearms and curl as my body revels in the throes of carnal passion.

"So responsive, mate. But we've only begun."

That's the only warning Jagger gives me before he withdraws to his tip, then snaps his hips forward to fill me to the root again. His heavy sac slaps my ass. I yelp and hold on tighter as the brutal force shifts my body up the mattress. Pillows cushion the sides of my head.

Jagger becomes a machine as his hips piston repeatedly. One of his arms bands around my waist as the palm of the other slams on the headboard. His solid torso flattens my breasts as he locks me to him for a mind-blowing ride.

"You are mine, Sage Waters. All mine," he growls against my ear. His warm breath sends a shudder through me. "Tell me you are mine!"

I gulp air into my mouth to refill my lungs.

"Answer me!" He bellows as his thrusts turn barbaric.

My pussy clamps down and gushes, so aroused every time he gets forceful with me. I did not know I would respond to such a rough manner. And I love it!

"Uh. Uh. Uh. Uh."

I can't verbalize too far gone for words. My body only feels his raw intensity—the demands he makes of it to accept his claim. I'm on the edge of the abyss and want oh so badly for him to mark me, make me his in every way.

Tears leak from the corners of my eyes. They land on his cheek, and he lifts his head to stare at me. He nods, realizing without me having to speak just what I feel—and need.

"Give in to us, Sage," Jagger says, emphasizing each word with a thrust and drag of his giant dick inside of my soaked and ravaged core. His eyes flash, and the wolf appears again. "MINE!!!"

He lowers his mouth to my neck.

 *agger*

SAGE'S TEARS trigger my wolf. I can no longer hold back. Nor deny what is ours to take. Our growls unite to form one all-encompassing word.

"MINE!!!"

I lower my head and nuzzle her neck. She mewls and turns her head to the side giving me better access to the juncture of her neck and shoulder. My cock swells at her submission and increases its pace to pound her into the mattress.

The serum to lodge my scent in her skin permanently and to enact the transformation of her into a wolf shifter drips on my extended canines. My gift to my fated mate, and Sage Waters will be my mate forever. We can never part once I issue the claiming bite. Or I truly would go crazy and lose control of my wolf. Or worse.

My thick fingers circle her slim throat like a collar to lock her in place. It will be painful, and I don't want her to jerk away, potentially causing damage from my canines. Add in Sage isn't a wolf shifter capable of healing immediately, and a misplaced claiming bite can prove dangerous.

I angle my thrusts to hit her G-spot, ensuring optimal pleasure. It triggers an orgasm for my fated mate. As she screams my name in carnal passion, my canines sink into her delicate flesh. Her moan morphs into a pained cry. Instinctively, she tries to pull away from me. But I tighten my grip on her throat and rumble in my chest to soothe her.

My mouth gapes, and I bite down again with an added shake of my head. The bite must be deep enough and fill her with an ample amount of serum. She writhes beneath me as pleasure from my pounding cock overtakes the pain of my claiming bite.

Her moans trigger my release.

A tingling at the base of my spine shoots to my balls and down my shaft, where my knot forms at its base. My mouth disengages from my fated mate's neck as my head lifts towards the ceiling. A victorious howl rings out as my knot locks her to me and the first ropes of my seed jettison inside of her womb.

My grip moves to cup her ass. Our groins melded together will not allow one drop of my seed to slip from her pussy, for I will put my pup inside of my fated mate this day. The rhythm of my strokes slow but doesn't stop as her greedy pussy milks every bit of my seed.

The stretch of her pussy by my knot causes her pain. She babbles incoherently as she clings to me.

I stare down at her, and my heart swells. Sage is the most beautiful being I've ever seen. She glows as though lit from within. A sheen of sweat coats her toffee-colored skin flush with her arousal. Long, silky strands of ebony curls stick to her neck or fan out around her head. A contented sigh slips past her Cupid's bow lips. I made her blissed out, I muse with a smirk.

My eyes land on the claiming bite. Saliva fills my mouth, and I lean down to lap at the wound. Properties in my saliva will help speed up the healing process. Now, we'll have to wait for the transformation to complete.

My knot remains embedded at her pussy entrance. I have no wish to break our intimate connection, even if I could. But her much smaller frame can't continue to bear my weight. I wrap an arm around her and roll onto my back. She snuggles her cheek against my chest with another sigh. My hand strokes from her back to her ass and up again as more rumbles vibrate from my chest to soothe my fated mate.

Sage Waters, my fated mate forever.

With that thought in mind, I drift off to a peaceful slumber.

I awake on my side wrapped around Sage with my erect cock nestled between the crack of her round ass. I groan as

I lean into her, wanting to envelop her with my body. Fuck! She feels so damn good. So right in my arms. Where she belongs.

I brush curls from her neck to stare at my mark. The indentations from my canines prove easily discernible. No one can mistake her for being unmated. I nuzzle against her soft skin and inhale deeply. My face splits into a grin at our combined scents. My wolf's feathery tail thumps in approval as he sits on his haunches guarding our mate.

"Jagger?"

"Yes, baby?"

I growl when she tries to slip from my grip. She giggles as she swats at one hand on her tit and the other cupping her pussy. She stills and moans when a thick finger slips between her slick folds, already wet for me. Her ass grinds back against my erection.

I seize the opportunity and flip her beneath me on her hands and knees—ass high, head low. A snap of my hips, and she mewls as my cock bottoms out inside her tight little pussy.

"You do not leave our bed without my permission, mate," I chide, cock plunging in and out with absolute precision. My torso lowers over her back to bring my lips close to her ear. "Or I will punish you soundly."

Her pussy clamps down and strangles my cock. We groan in unison.

I rear back up, dick still deep, and smack her ass. Left, right, right, left. Never in the same spot. Yet close enough to elicit a baby howl from my fated mate. I grin. Yeah, baby howl away.

My hand snakes around her hip and collects her juices. I rub her clit with her natural lube, and she cums with a scream. She bucks against my hand as her fingernails shred the sheets.

"Oh, Fates, Jagger!" She cries as her pussy squeezes the life out of me. "You're so big. Fuck!"

What a stroke to my ego.

I go all out with a punishing rhythm between my cock in her dripping pussy and my palm on her reddened ass cheeks. She writhes beneath me, screaming through one orgasm after the other. I mount her like the feral beast I am, then spill my seed deep within her womb, pussy locked to me by my knot.

I lower us to our sides as we catch our breath and heartbeats return to normal.

"Jagger, I wanted to go to the bathroom," Sage says accusingly.

I nuzzle her neck as I rumble. She sighs and relaxes against me.

"You wild boy… Don't think your little sounds will hold my bladder."

I chuckle, and she joins in. Moments later, soft snores let me know she's asleep again. With my fated mate wrapped in my arms, I close my eyes, sated.

～

Sage

SUNLIGHT DAPPLES THE STILL, *smooth surface of the pond. No wind whispers through the saw grass along its rim. A great egret spreads its snowy white wings as it silently takes to the sky. It glances down at me as if to say, you should leave too, if you know what's best. Instead, I watch it fly into the distance.*

I return to my walk. The Everglades give me peace and tranquility. A place I retreat to when my mother's demands of perfection drive me crazy. I shake my head to dispel the bad vibes in my special place, then slip a loose ebony curl behind my ear with a sigh.

But as I continue along the path between the pine trees, the hairs on the back of my neck rise. I don't change my pace. Instead, I focus on my surroundings, now eerily silent, as though a predator lurks. My ears pick up the silent tread of a four-legged creature. One that appears to be stalking me.

My direction detours from the close proximity of the pine trees back to the open expanse surrounding the pond. The water remains without a ripple. Even the insects quiet as I approach. Whatever follows scares all.

But not me.

I pivot quickly to face the four-legged creature I sense will follow me into the open, unafraid of me or of anything else. I expect a Florida panther creeping behind me. They're known for their stealth and preference to bite the back of a person's neck to break the spine. Face-to-face, I'll have a better chance at defending myself against the lethal predator.

My eyes widen at the sight of a ginormous wolf as it pads into the clearing. Its silvery white coat gleams in the early morning sun. Ice blue eyes should freeze me. Instead, they send a frisson of carnal heat through my body. A tremor follows in its wake. My mouth falls slack on a gasp.

Instinctively, I know it's a male wolf. But unlike any regular wolf. Although beautiful unto themselves, this wolf is majestic. The most incredible thing I've ever seen—and I've seen all kinds of stuff.

He lopes towards me with nostrils flared as he scents the air. His formidable size brings his massive head nearly to my shoulder, where I stand at five feet, five inches. Only needing to tip his head up slightly, his eyes remain locked on mine.

In their icy depths, I see a hunger—and not to devour my flesh. A yearning that tugs at my heart and zings my core. A low rumbling from the depths of his broad chest washes over me. Instantly, my body releases the tension built from his unexpected appearance. My eyes flutter closed as I sway.

Warm wetness and silky fur on the side of my neck stills my movement as my eyes pop open. I gasp. My heartbeat slams against my ribcage, frightened by the nearness of his exposed canines to my delicate neck.

I take a step back.

He rumbles and matches my movement.

My heel catches on a rock, and I fall on my ass. I swear I see a flicker of laughter in his eyes as he steps between my legs. On their own, my bent knees butterfly to the ground to allow him closer access. He stands above me and once again nuzzles my neck, inhaling deeply.

This time, I mewl when his textured tongue swipes my sensitive skin. My nipples pucker against the thin cotton of my white t-shirt. I cry out as my core moistens and clenches with need. Then yelp when his nose nudges the front of my black leggings, flush against the apex of my thighs.

A low growl emanates from his mouth as he drags his ice blue eyes up my quivering belly, lingers on my heaving chest, and stops at my flushed face. He licks his muzzle from one side to the other as though he tastes me on his tongue. Another low growl sends a shiver down my spine. His pheromones waft around us, matching my arousal.

A crackling sound and a flash appear.

I blink.

A gorgeous male stares at me. A naked, muscular, gorgeous male stares at me. As my eyes travel the length of his body, I notice his giant dick thumps his eight-pack abs. A pearl of pre-cum glistens from the slit of its bulbous tip.

I close my eyes. Too much to take in for a virgin like me.

"Mine!"

His rough growl snaps me back.

My eyes open and meet his.

His gaze dip to my chest, then back at my face. A hint of a smirk plays at the corners of his lush mouth. His fingers grip the collar of my t-shirt. With the flick of his wrists, he rips it from neck to hem. The soft bra rends in two to expose my breasts to his lust-filled gaze.

My lips part on a whimper.

His mouth crashes onto mine. That same wicked tongue

sweeps inside, demanding my tongue tangle with his. I comply. The low rumbling increases and vibrates on my heated skin.

I cry out, but his mouth swallows my plea.

Whether a plea for him to stop or to claim me as his, I'm not sure. What I know without a doubt is this wolf shifter intends to have his way with me, his captured prey. I shudder as his mouth leaves mine to trail licks and nips across my jaw and down to the column of my neck.

The press of his canines against my throat draws another yelp from me. He rumbles to soothe me once again. I relax as he continues his carnal path over my collarbone and down to my heavy breasts. The achy nipples beg for his sinful mouth to engulf them.

He does.

His tongue curls around one distended tip to suck it into his wet, warm mouth. He flicks his tongue over the tightened bud as his mouth widens to take in more of my ample breast. Savage snarls and grunts issue from his mouth as he feasts on my breast, moving from one to the other and back again.

I writhe beneath him as my fingernails dig into his broad back. My core fills with my slick arousal, drenched and ready for him to claim me completely. To take that gigantic dick and mark my virgin body as his and his alone.

My wetness must call to him since he leaves my sore nipples to skim his lips over my flat belly and down to my mons. The forceful rip of fabric precedes his hot mouth on my most vulnerable flesh. My back bows and my hips rise on a scream as he licks from my slick slit to my engorged clit.

Sizable, calloused hands press my hips down to the soft

ground. Fingers slip around to grip each butt cheek as his wide shoulders press my trembling thighs apart. Settled in place, he devours me.

Lusty grunts mingle with the squelching of my abundant juices to fill the surrounding air. Even I can scent my arousal as my head tosses side to side and desperate moans pour from my mouth. I want more. I want that dick!

But locked in place by his powerful hands, I can only lie there and take what he gives to me.

A tingle builds in my lower belly and spreads through me. My breath hitches in my throat. My core tightens as my toes curl, still inside of my hiking boots. Sight and sound disappear as the wave of a massive orgasm crests.

I scream until hoarse as wave after wave knocks into me. My body convulses and my eyes roll to the back of my head. My fingers claw at his long, white blond hair. Whether they mean to pull him away or bring him closer remains unclear. My mind too blown by the deep-seated throes of my first non-self-induced orgasm.

Between gulps of my gushing core, he raises those magnetic ice blue eyes to my hooded emerald green gaze. He rumbles, and the vibrations from his chest skitter across my heated skin, leaving goosebumps in their wake.

"Mine!"

With his eyes still locked on me, he takes a last lick of my swollen lower lips and crawls up my body. The corded muscles of his arms and shoulders flex beneath his skin.

I inhale deeply, knowing what comes next. He'll claim my virgin flesh as his own.

Planked over me, he nuzzles my neck, sending ripples of erotic energy along my spine. His lips brush my earlobe as he murmurs, "Mine."

He reaches between us to grip his turgid length and align it with my core. His eyes find mine—

"Jagger! I remember! I remember everything!"

CHAPTER 10

 *agger*

"Yeah, baby! You got it, Sage! Fly, baby, fly!!"

I yell through the megaphone as I stand on *Moonbeam*'s aft deck.

My fated mate zips past me with her feet strapped in special boots that use a propulsion mechanism from the jet ski guiding her flyboarding experience. It's her second time doing the extreme sport and the first session of our trip. She's become good at it in a short time because of her increased strength—one difference her body has experienced in the last few days since her transformation began. She swears she's not using her magick to control the water.

I'm not so sure since it seems to carry her along. I shake my head and chuckle.

A grin and thumbs-up serve as my fated mate's response.

I grin even more than she does as I watch her plump ass in a red string bikini bottom when she passes the boat. A life jacket covers her lush D-cup tits. I'd have to chew out the eyes of the crew should a tit pop out of her string bikini top from the jostling of the powerful propulsion. Only mine!

My wolf nods his massive head in agreement. When she first stepped off the boat, he whined, concerned for her safety. I assured him our mate was fine. Now he watches her—and the crew—intently. Ready to spring forward to rescue her.

How quickly she healed from my claiming bite surprised us. We were even more shocked by how it triggered the return of her memories. All of them. We spent hours talking as we sat in bed, and I fed her meals. She admitted she wanted more then but was afraid of what her mother would do. Well, now we know the lengths our parents took to keep Sage and me apart for ten years. Fuck!

She sensed my anger and soothed me with kisses all over my face until I fell back against the pillows with laughter and allowed her to ravage me. The one time I let her take the lead in our lovemaking. As an Alpha male, to give up control is beyond my comprehension. But I spoil my fated mate. I've been too long without her to not let her have her fun. Plus, the pleasure is mutually conducive. My wolf nods, with his tongue lolling from his mouth in agreement enthusiastically.

My only concern is she hasn't shifted yet. She tells me her magick may block the ability. We won't know until more time passes. I know wolf shifters whose human mates' transformation didn't give them the ability to shift. But my wolf aches to run with hers. We'll just have to wait and see.

Tomorrow is Sage's birthday. We return to Miami the next morning. My stomach churns. I shake off the negative thoughts as I remind myself I am Alpha of my pack, and they will obey or pay the price. Sage is their Luna, and they better respect her.

We have talked little on the subject of what happens when we return. My plan is for her to move into our mansion on Moon Island. Immediately. We can have our mate bonding ceremony to complete our mating. If she wants a wedding too, we can do it then or at a later date. But we will have the ceremony now. Whomever isn't for our mating can go fly a fucking kite—my parents and hers included.

I bring my attention back to Sage. She laughs as she flies higher and higher, carried by the propulsion. She signals the crew member on the jet ski, and he brings her down to the water's surface. I dive in and channel my inner Michael Phelps to reach her in a few powerful strokes.

"That was incredible! I can't wait to do it again!" Sage enthuses, floating on her back as I take the boots from her feet and hand them to the crew member. "I could go all day, but I'm hungry."

I chuckle and cup her face. My mouth descends on hers for a toe-curling kiss as we tread water. I can't get enough of my fated mate—of us. It's been perfect. I couldn't ask for anything more.

Her arms wrap around my neck as she returns my kiss with a fiery passion of her own. My cock hardens in my board shorts. She feels it and lifts her legs to draw me close to her body. Her hand reaches between us, and she frees my cock, then aligns it with her pussy.

"But I'm more hungry for you, Jagger Larson," she purrs against my lips.

I growl and thrust forward, breaching her folds in one swift motion. Her tight pussy encases my cock from root to tip. My eyelids close to absorb the carnal sensation. Her pussy walls flutter as they expand to take in every one of my thick inches. I groan in pleasure.

My fated mate proves to be insatiable. Always wet and ready for me to take her, no matter how rough or gentle. And I'm more than willing to oblige her needs.

As I do now. I band my arms around her and pump up into her pussy. The water churns from my powerful thrusts. Her soft cries like a red flag to a bull. I must take her. All else fades—the crew, the boat, the world.

"Oh, Fates, Jagger!" She screams as she cums undone so beautifully for me. Her pussy clenches on my cock, and she wails.

I'm right with her and throw my head back for an

earth-shaking roar. My seed floods her pussy like a geyser. She shakes uncontrollably as her orgasm rocks throughout her body. Since we're in the water, I suppress my knot. With a groan, I slip out of her pussy. I kiss her mouth like a possessed male before I urge her back to *Moonbeam*.

She all but glides on the surface ahead of me. Yeah, she used her magick. I follow along at a slower pace.

Once we're back on board, I dip down and put my shoulder into her midsection to put her over my shoulder. Sage giggles and slaps my ass. I return the love tap with a few smacks to her ass. She yelps and wiggles it. Another thing I learned, Sage loves punishment. I won't go so far as a pain slut, but she's a natural submissive. I can't wait to get her to Club Sol & Mani. Explore more of her sub side as her Dom and to introduce her to the BDSM lifestyle. I grin as I carry my fated-mate-cum-sub up the stairs to the outdoor dining deck for lunch.

"I can walk, you know," she says when I put her on her feet by a chair. "No need to carry me about like a sack of potatoes, Jagger."

I nuzzle her neck and murmur, "You're too gorgeous to be a plain old sack of potatoes, Sage, mate of mine."

She giggles and swats at me with a linen napkin as she sits. I round the table and sit across from her. The Chief Stew appears with ceviche for our appetizer. The Stewardess fills our wineglasses with a chilled rosé. We thank them.

"You're welcome, Alpha, Luna," they chime in unison.

Sage blushes at the acknowledgment the crew adopted

since they spied my claiming bite on her neck. Bikinis and strapless maxi dresses do nothing to hide my claim of my fated mate. I smirk as I lift a spoonful of ceviche to her lips.

At first, she complained about me feeding her. After a few spankings, she learned her lesson and takes her meals from my hand without issue. I sense she enjoys it. Again, a natural sub. And I love it. In fact, I love her more than life itself.

I haven't spoken the words yet. But I will tomorrow.

Sage

"HAPPY BIRTHDAY, MATE."

I lift my arms overhead and stretch my muscles, sore from countless hours of lovemaking over these past few days. I turn my head and open my eyes to find Jagger on an elbow staring down at me. The expression of love so raw on his handsome face, my heart constricts. Neither of us has said those three words. Although our bodies shouted them for us again and again. I smile and cup his face.

"Thank you, Jagger," I respond.

It's still hard for me to say mate, and I know he notices but hasn't mentioned it. We are fated mates, with no doubt. However, I worry still. Before I can delve into negative thoughts, Jagger moves over me.

His forearms bracket my head with his palms cradling its crown. Ice blue eyes scan my face before he lowers his full mouth to mine. The kiss is slow and touches every inch inside my mouth until his tongue teases mine to join with him. I do.

Breathless and toes curled later, he pulls back to gaze at me. I raise an eyebrow questioningly.

"I love you, Sage Waters,"

My heart skips a beat.

"I love you so much it hurts. I've never felt this way before. Other than ten years ago. I'm so thankful to the Fates they brought us together again, baby."

He reaches under his pillow and pulls out a little black velvet box. His gaze flicks back to me before he pushes the sapphire cabochon closure. Nestled in a black suede pillow, a gigantic pear-shaped diamond ring winks at me. The sunlight through the cabin's windows shines on the platinum-set stone for a dazzling display of rainbows.

I gasp.

"You are my fated mate, Sage Waters. No one else will ever do for me. You bound my heart the moment I spied you in the Everglades ten years ago. You took my heart then. Now. I've given you my claiming bite and here is my ring—a family heirloom. We will complete our bonding with the mate bonding ceremony and a wedding, if you wish."

His sincerity proves my undoing.

I fling my arms around his neck and bury my face against his skin. I inhale his masculine scent as I pray we can get through the challenges we'll face once we return to Miami.

He must sense my stress and rocks his cock into my core. I sigh and spread my legs to give him full access. I need him to take me. To remind me I am his and his alone and no one can separate us as they did ten years ago.

Our lovemaking is full of passion as we lose ourselves in the other. As we cum as one, I cry out his name.

"Jagger! I love you."

age

Why are you being so tight-lipped? Where are you?

You have your last fitting for your wedding gown? Where are you?

HELLOOOOOOOOOO...

Sage, what's up? I'm coming to Miami sooner. I can't believe you're not telling me, your bestie, what's going on.

Sage! Rupert is going crazy trying to contact you! You haven't even told your fiancé where you are? Come on already...

I SCROLL through many text messages from my sisters and Anala while Jagger and I ride in the tender back to the marina.

Before we left, I sent a text message to Willow—who, as the second oldest—stands in for me in my absence. I didn't give her a reason I was taking five days off. Only that I would be unreachable unless it was an emergency. I've never taken time from my duties. So, I don't feel bad about dropping out of reach. Besides, my connection to our coven would alert me to any danger. However, I increased the wards as a precaution.

The sense of peace from the few days of happiness Jagger and I shared blows away like dandelion pappus on the breeze. In its place, the original reasons we can't be together resurface. The tension creeps up my spine like a frigid chill. I shiver despite the ninety-degree weather and sunshine streaming around us.

I allowed myself to indulge in what our life together could be like if not for Jagger being a wolf shifter and me a witch. His pack and my coven won't stand for our mating. I can empathize with Juliet on a deeper level, not just feeling sorry for her and her forbidden lover.

"What's wrong?"

Jagger's question as he wraps a powerful arm around my shoulders pulls me from my musings. He leans over to peer at the mobile screen. A low, feral growl makes me shiver.

"I don't give a fuck how 'Rupert is going crazy.' I forbid you to see him. Enrique can return the ring," Jagger says with finality as he sits back, arms folded over his massive chest, and stares ahead.

My mouth opens, then closes, unsure of what to say. I can't simply have someone else return the ring. This calls for a conversation. One held in person. It's already bad enough. Plus, I bear Jagger's claiming bite and ring a day before my wedding to Rupert. I don't want to cause further ripples in my coven's relationship with his coven, especially since it's the second most powerful.

How the hell do I tell Jagger?

He'll never go along with me meeting Rupert alone. And I cannot allow Jagger to be present. What a mess that would become!

So, I remain quiet as I go back to my text messages. I don't respond to them yet. What's mentioned will give me a heads up to what I'll face when I return to The Waters Tower. The first instance that caused Jagger's ire.

He wants me to move in with him now. I told him I need to settle things with the wedding. Of course, he went all possessive and snarly. But I didn't back down. I must do it my way.

The tender pulls up to the dock, and a crew member hops onto it to secure the line before we disembark. Jagger gets out and extends his hand to me. I glance up at him, nervous at what I may find. His unreadable expression makes me hesitate until he cocks an eyebrow. I nod, more to convince myself I'm doing the right thing than to acknowledge his questioning gaze. My hand slips into his, and he pulls me to stand before him, held tight to his body.

I lift my gaze to meet his eyes, hidden by sunglasses. I chew on the corner of my lower lip knowing he's about to freak out. Again, I press on. I stand on tiptoe and brush my lips against his chin, the closest spot I can reach.

"I'm not running away. I told you I have to go."

As Jagger shimmers, he squeezes me closer and growls for me not to go. Then he fades away. His anguished howl pierces the absolute depths of my soul.

I land on the bed in my penthouse duplex. Immediately, I sense his loss. My arms wrap around my body at the sudden chill. I close my eyes to focus on my inner strength and inhale deeply. With an exhalation, I sit up and stride to my en suite bathroom for a shower.

Dressed in a wrap dress with a silk scarf tied around my neck artfully and sky-high strappy sandals, I leave my bedroom for part one of my task. I shoot a text message to Willow, Lillie, and Anala asking them to meet me in my coven offices.

Not a second passes before their responses come through and my mobile rings. I ignore the text messages and send the call to voicemail. Instead, I use my teleportation magick to enter my offices, determined to get this part finished ASAP.

Situated on the floor below Lillie's penthouse, my coven offices share the vast space with Willow's office, several conference rooms, and our coven's grand hall.

Anala has the ability to teleport, but not within our coven's wards. So, I have time before my girls arrive.

With that in mind, I send a text message to my fated mate.

I'm at The Waters Tower. Please don't be mad. I have to do this my way. I love you. xo S

I blink and the three dots show he's texting a response.

You should have let me come with you. I am not pleased with your decision, Sage. I do not want you anywhere near that witch.

I hear my girls before my door opens. Quickly, I respond.

Please, Jagger.

I close the app while the three dots appear and stand, a hand pressed against my aching heart.

"Sage! What the hell?!"

"You are *so* wrong for not answering not one of us, Sage!"

"Sage, what's going on?"

I remove my hand from my chest and gesture towards the sitting area. My sisters settle on the chairs, and I sit beside Anala on the sofa. Their eyes focus on me. I nod.

"I cannot marry Rupert—"

"What?!"

"Seriously?!"

"What's going on?"

I raise my hand to stop their onslaught of questions. Once they quiet down, I speak.

"Jagger Larson Alpha of the Miami Wolves Pack is my fated mate."

An uproar ensues. I sit back and wait for them to clear their systems. They notice my silent reaction to their shouts of denial and shut up. I continue.

"I cannot marry Rupert."

I wait out more screeches of disbelief.

"Is that why you wear the scarf, Sage?"

Naturally, Anala—who's the wisest of the three—asks as she flicks her gaze between my neck and my eyes. My sisters gasp. Lillie jumps up and tugs at the scarf. It unwinds from my neck to reveal the marks left by Jagger's canines. She covers her mouth with a trembling hand.

"Sage… no…" she cries as her eyes widen. She glances at her twin for support.

Willow jumps from her chair to get a closer look. She shakes her head and sighs.

"Sage, you know it can't work out between a wolf shifter and a witch. Especially you, Sage. What the hell were you thinking?!"

She returns to her chair and plops down with her eyes closed, as though the sight of Jagger's claiming bite proves too much for her. Lillie follows suit with a sigh.

Anala watches all but says nothing.

I clap my hands and lean forward to pin each of them with an intense stare.

"Okay, now that we're past the news… I need to know if Jagger and I will have your support or not. I will not pressure you in any way. However, know this… I would support you no matter what, especially for a fated mate. We cannot know the reason the Fates pair couples. We can only go by what they decree or suffer from the loss of the fated mate. And I will tell you, being here with you and not with Jagger pains me more than I thought possible."

They exchange anxious glances. The Twins connect on a deeper level. One can see their internal dialogue play out. I wait patiently for their answers, knowing I will continue with or without their support. It would be better to have them on my side when I inform Rupert, then the coven.

"How sure are you of being fated mates?" Anala breaks the silence.

"Absolutely. Ten years ago, Jagger and I first met and realized our connection. Mother and his father found us, and Mother cast spells to erase our memories despite us telling them we're fated mates," I say, then pause to gauge their reactions.

Willow sits forward with her eyebrows raised.

Lillie's mouth drops open.

Anala nods her head, neither surprised nor concerned. Again, she speaks first.

"How could Aunt Prudence use her magick against you?" Anala's eyebrows raise surprised my mother can use her magick against a family member.

I sigh before I respond, "She didn't tell me. But I'll figure it out."

"So, if you lost your memories, how is it you know now—"

"Wait a minute! Is that who kidnapped you from the club?!" Anala leaps to her feet as her question cuts Lillie off.

"That wolf shifter who carried you away and drove off with you?!"

Her eyes burn molten chocolate with her inner fire as she stares at me. Her fingers twitch as though she holds her two curved blades. Undoubtedly because of her reliving Jagger carrying me over his shoulder out of the club and ignoring her at his car's window.

"Yes, he is the one. That night, he caught the scent of his fated mate, and it combated the spell. His memories returned, and he sought me out. My memories returned after he issued his claiming bite."

"Well, damn," Anala says as she falls back to the sofa. "You have my support, Sage. But he better not mess up."

I smile at my bestie, then turn to my sisters.

"Fine," The Twins say in unison.

Lillie sits up with wide eyes and asks, "Oh, Sage! Does Mother know?"

Anala and Willow turn to me.

I nod and relay the encounter in my parents' penthouse duplex. My girls sit enraptured, then confirm they're still with me despite my parents' reaction. Pleased, I hug each of them before I move to part two of my task. Rupert.

"Sage, darling, I was so worried about you! Where have you been?"

I turn my head as Rupert leans over to kiss my lips. His

mouth glances off my cheek. A frown mars his handsome face as he settles in the chair opposite mine.

"Are you all right, Sage?"

I nod and clear my throat.

"I'm fine. No need to worry, Rupert. Shall we order?" I respond as I lift a menu to ignore his deepening scowl. "I recommend their chicken paillard with arugula and tomatoes. It's tasty. The server can go over the specials, if you prefer."

He's silent as he studies my face. His obsidian eyes narrow at the scarf around my neck. A second later, he cocks his head as his nostrils flare. A slow breath leaves him.

"Sage, am I mistaken, or do I smell a male wolf shifter on you?"

Rupert's question doesn't surprise me.

Wolf shifters are not the only beings with heightened senses. Which is the reason I attempted to mask Jagger's scent embedded in me. My girls didn't take note of it. But a male—as intended—will detect another male's scent on a female. However, I had hoped to get further along in lunch and our conversation before Rupert noticed.

Aargh!

"Rupert, we need to talk," I respond, then stop when the server appears at the table. I wait for her to complete the list of specials while Rupert stares at me, transfixed. When she leaves, I return his gaze. "Shall we continue our conversation here or upstairs?"

I wanted to meet with him surrounded by others. But it's best to avoid a public scene.

Without a word, Rupert rises, places his napkin on the table, and comes around to help me from my chair. A smidgen of hope unfurls in my belly. Perhaps this will go better than I expected. He places a palm on my lower back to guide me from the restaurant.

We move in silence through The Waters Tower Mall to the separate entry for the residences. I try to slip from Rupert's hold—as subtle as it is—unsuccessfully. Each time, he moves closer and applies more pressure. The tension in the private elevator is palpable.

I glance from beneath the thick fringe of my eyelashes at him in the reflection of the doors. He remains impassive.

We step out into the entry foyer of my penthouse duplex. I place my hand on the plaque, and the lock disengages. Rupert reaches around to hold the doors for me. I duck under his arm, careful not to touch him in an intimate way.

"Would you care for a drink?" I ask as I move towards the living room. My heels click on the marble tile. The only sound in the space rings loud in my ears.

"Sage, you're not wearing my ring. What is going on?"

I turn to face Rupert. He remains by the doors. Enough with this dance. I take a deep breath and reach inside of my Bottega Veneta woven clutch. I hold out his ring as I answer him with sincerity.

"Rupert, I became aware of my fated mate again after ten years, during which they concealed our memories from us. Had I known, I would have called off the pairing between you and me years ago. I'm sure this news comes as a surprise to you as it did for me. But I sincerely hope you understand and harbor no ill will towards me, my fated mate, and my coven. If the roles were reversed, I would not stand in the way of you and the destiny the Fates put forth."

He stares at the ring, then lifts his blank obsidian eyes to my face.

I find it unsettling he shows no reaction. As I open my mouth to speak, he steps forward and plucks the ring from my palm as he responds.

"Sage, you are correct. I would never have expected this news," Rupert starts, then he draws up even taller than his six feet, six inches. "I cannot deny your belief in the Fates. Therefore, we must call off the pairing and make our covens aware. Most of the guests arrived yesterday. A message should suffice. I expect you will handle the situation while I return to New York. I doubt anyone will linger to interfere in your newfound happiness. And I suppose you are happy, Sage?"

I nod, then verbalize a positive response.

He inclines his head.

"Well, then I bid you farewell, Sage Waters."

Rupert pivots and strides out the doors.

I hurry after him. The elevator doors close as our eyes connect. Once again, he shrouds his emotions. A shudder runs through me. But I shake it off.

My hope is it ends here.

agger

"I GET IT, bro. But you can't start a war with her witch fiancé—"

My ferocious growl cuts Tag off. My beta raises his hands, palms out, head bowed in submission. He chances my wrath by continuing.

"No disrespect, Alpha. But we have to be strategic and not let our emotions come into play. I can't say I know what it's like to have my fated mate away from me *and* with another male. However, I get your need to protect what is yours. I suggest we go to The Waters Tower and see if we can get word to her through the doorman. I doubt we can pass through the protective wards to enter the building."

I study Tag with narrowed eyes. What he says makes sense. But the pain caused by separation from my fated mate wrenching through me muddles my thought process. My wolf and I can only focus on getting to our fated mate and ripping out that witch fucker's throat.

"Alpha?"

Tag's question brings me back from blood-thirsty visions of a shredded *Rupert*.

My beta speaks the truth. I nod and growl for the two of us and my security team to leave Moon Island. On the way, I call Sage's mobile only for it to go straight to voicemail. With a snarl, my fingers fly across my mobile screen as I type a text message.

I am on my way. You cannot stop me.

The sound of splintering glass fills the inside of my SUV as the grip on my mobile threatens to crush it. I loosen it at Tag's cocked eyebrow, then slam myself back against the supple leather seat. My eyes close as I try to temper the beast inside of me.

"We're here, Alpha."

My eyes pop open, and I reach for the door handle. It opens from the outside by Karl, the head of my security team. His eyes scan the area as I jump from the SUV to the sidewalk in front of The Waters Tower. My head goes back as I inhale deeply, hoping to catch a whiff of my fated mate. Nothing. I growl low in my chest and prowl towards the doorman.

It's the same one as the other day. A flicker of recognition crosses his face, then he raises his guard as he eyes me and the wolf shifters behind me. The doorman stands taller and squares his shoulders, ready to defend his High Witch.

Fuck him.

"I know you remember me with Sage Waters. I need to get a message to her. Now."

The doorman doesn't even flinch at my command. He shakes his head and tells me no.

Tag's hand shoots out and grabs my arm as I lift it to throttle the fucker in front of me. Then his eyes show a bit of fear as he sees my wolf leap to the surface and alter my appearance. The fucker trembles visibly and backs away towards the doors.

"Hey! What's going on here?!"

I whirl around, eyes flashing sapphire barely containing to my wolf. He paces and snarls with canines bared as his tail flicks back and forth. He's eager to get past the doorman and to our fated mate.

"Move out of my way!"

I step from behind my security team to find the source of the angry voice. My eyes widen at the sight of a female witch with chocolate brown eyes ablaze as though an internal fire fuels them. Her mane of ebony curls swirls around her head by the power that emanates from her body. She's a powerful one. And she's the one from the club —Sage's friend. She can help us.

The witch's fiery glower lands on me. Her eyes narrow as her lip curls.

"You! You owe me an apology," she says, arching an eyebrow as her arms fold beneath her breasts.

My men growl. She pins each of them with a death glare, then cocks her head at me. Lips pursed, she waits for my response.

My wolf gnashes his teeth. But in a flash of clarity, I realize this witch is the only hope I have of getting to my fated mate. It will pay to make the witch a friend and not a foe. I tell my men to back down as I approach her.

She throws her head back and laughs throatily. Then she glares at each of them and me.

"You think I need your help, wolf shifter? I am a skilled *vampire* hunter. They nor *you* frighten me in any way," she scoffs. "Now, apologize or move."

I bite back a retort. She smirks at my inner struggle. The heat in her eyes softens to a glow full of mirth. Okay, she's a badass. But she's not fucking with me out of spite. She's testing me. Fine.

"I apologize for my behavior towards you at the club"— her smirk widens, but I hold up my hand—"However, I will never apologize for taking my fated mate."

The witch scans my face for any artifice. Finding none, she nods.

"Apology accepted, Larson. I already pledged my support of your pairing to my cousin and best friend"— now she holds up her hand to stop me from speaking— "However, should you hurt Sage in any way, I will end you. Period."

Tag tenses beside me. But I wave him and the others off.

She has every right to say what she said. I respect her honesty and loyalty. Not to mention she supports Sage and me. A valuable advocate for us to have on our side. I incline my head to the witch, and she smiles.

Then her eyes widen as she stares over my shoulder.

I spin around. Through the glass exterior of The Tower, a tall male with jet black hair walks beside a woman with his hand on her lower back. The couple heads towards an elevator.

Fuck. Me.

My vision tunnels on them as they step through the elevator doors. The sound of rending fabric fills the air. My wolf breaks free in an instant. We charge forward only to bounce back and land on our rump. My massive head shakes, and we rush ahead.

"Larson, you cannot get past the barrier I erected. You must calm down and shift back."

My wolf and I round on the witch.

She stands within a circle of fire, two flaming curved swords in each of her hands.

"I will help you. So, do not make me use my powers against you and your men. Do you understand?"

My wolf growls, hackles raised, and flicks his feathery tail. I glance around and notice people walk past us as though we do not exist. They don't bump into the barrier nor notice the circle of fire within it. Tag and my men dart their gazes between the witch and me. I throw my head back and let loose an anguished howl, then force my wolf to retreat. He snarls but obeys while he paces on the fringes, ready to come forth anew.

"Great, now how the hell do we enter the building with

you buck naked, Larson?" The witch giggles as she covers her eyes with a dainty hand free of the sword. "And I have no interest in seeing my bestie's mate's family jewels. Eww!"

Tag chuckles as he instructs one man to get the extra clothes we keep in the SUV for times like this one. The witch waves her hand.

"Never mind, I'll take care of it. You need to look sharp and make a good impression as we enter The Tower," she says as a well-tailored, three-piece suit and the appropriate accessories cover me. "Oh, and I'm Anala Azar of the Northeast Coven, by the way."

"Thank you, Anala, nice to meet you officially," I say with a smirk, then introduce her to Tag and my men.

She nods, and the barrier disappears. "Shall we?"

We follow her inside. As much as my wolf wants to snap at the doorman, I maintain a stoic expression as we pass him, holding the door. He mumbles a greeting to Anala. She nods but doesn't slow her pace.

And she is correct. The witches who come and go in the lobby eyeball our group as we walk to the elevator. Some stare openly while others ogle surreptitiously at us. Their whispered exclamations clear with my wolf senses. The others give her and us a wide berth. I follow Anala's lead and ignore them.

"Now, listen to me carefully and swear you will not lose control again. And that goes for all of you. Or I will invoke a spell you will regret," Anala says while we wait for the elevator. When we affirm our agreement, she continues. "I will take you to Sage's sister Willow's penthouse, one floor below Sage's residence. Then I will reach out to Sage and let her know we are here. It will be up to her to come get you."

My mind envisions all the things that fucker *Rupert* can do to my fated mate while we wait. A growl rises from my chest. As though reading my mind, Anala speaks again.

"Listen, I understand, Larson. But I know Sage. She will not allow Rupert to do anything untoward. She made it crystal clear to me and to her sisters *you* are her fated mate. All three of us support her and you. Do this my way. Trust me," she says fervently.

"Fine," I bite out.

She offers me a smile and steps onto the elevator. I must say, the male who captures this spitfire will be one lucky bastard. Beauty, strength, loyalty, compassion, all admirable traits in a mate. I wonder if the Fates could favor a male from my pack. Anala's laughter confirms she can read my mind. I grin back at her as the elevator doors close.

Soon we step off to an entry foyer. The double doors fly open, and two witches run out.

"What's going on?!"

"Does Sage know?"

I do a double take and realize they're identical twins who resemble Sage. They must be her sisters. I offer them a smile as Anala bustles them back inside and beckons for us to follow.

She recaps the events as I pace the living room. My

patience hangs on by a wolf's hair. The twins turn to me as one.

"You better be good to our sister…"

"Or we will use every ounce of our power to make you suffer unimaginable torture for all eternity."

Damn. Even my wolf shudders at their vow.

"I love Sage and will do nothing to hurt my fated mate. That I swear," I respond wholeheartedly.

"We will hold you to your word, Jagger Larson, Alpha of the Miami Wolves Pack," the twins state in unison.

"So will I."

My wolf leaps to his feet, tongue lolling from his mouth as he wags his tail and whines. I whirl around to find my fated mate behind me. Two long strides and she's in my arms, my face buried in her neck. I inhale deeply to check for the other male's scent on her. Only a trace from being in his presence, no lasting impact. Thank the Fates!

"I see you met my sisters Willow and Lillie and my cousin Anala again," Sage says with a laugh. "And believe me, they mean what they say. So, don't mess up, Jagger Larson."

"I won't," I answer gruffly, then pull back to stare down at her. "What happened with him?"

She shrugs and leads me to the sofa. She waits for everyone to sit, then recaps their conversation. When I growl at certain parts, she squeezes my hand and smiles at me reassuringly.

At the end, I don't trust the fucker. I glance at Tag. He nods, understanding I want eyes on *Rupert*. Our pack has close ties to the New York one. So, we'll have their support once I speak to their Alpha. I add the conversation as a mental note and tune back into my fated mate.

"—a message to the wedding guests and speak with the coven. I need to get those tasks completed right away. I don't want word to spread before I get a handle on the situation. Anala, I'll need you to gauge the New York coven's reaction. Will you return home now?"

Anala agrees and gives Sage and the twins hugs before she smirks at me and leaves the penthouse.

I can't help but to admire her fearlessness.

"Sage, I wrote a letter for you to provide the guests after you told us the wedding was called off permanently. Here, let me get it for you," the twin named Lillie says as she leaves the living room.

While she's gone, Sage instructs Willow to call the coven for a meeting in two hours. I grumble to myself, not wanting to wait any longer to get her home. But also glad she's taking care of things with a quickness. I hope it goes smoothly.

Lillie returns, and Sage makes a few changes to the letter. By Sage's magick, she disperses it to each person. They decide to make one for coven members unable to attend the last-minute meeting.

A little over an hour later, Sage and I enter her penthouse duplex. While we go up to her bedroom suite, Tag and my men go to the living room. As soon as the door shuts behind us, I spin her around and pin her to it.

My fingers untie the belt of her dress. The silk slips

open to reveal her lush curves. D-cups fill a black lace bra. Her flat belly leads to hips with the strings from her black lace G-string around them. I yank the cups down and lower my mouth to feast on her plump brown nipples.

She mewls as I lap at one. It tightens beneath my tongue. I flick the distended tip, then nip it. The bite of pain makes her back arc from the door as her fingers dive into my hair.

I pull back with a pop from her tit. With a flick of my wrist, the dress falls to the floor. I use the belt to bind her wrists. I open the door and toss the end over the top, then close it. Sage hangs suspended, arms overhead, toes wiggle to reach the floor. I step back to admire my work.

Her chest heaves as she pants and stares back at me with hooded eyes. Fingers flex into fists, grasping at the air. My ring on her finger sparkles with each movement. She squirms while a crimson hue licks along her breasts as I continue to watch her body react to the restraint.

"My beautiful, fated mate. Mine!"

I grip her hips and crush her mouth with mine. My tongue pushes past her lips and sweeps through her mouth. I groan at her sweet taste. Her tongue probes mine, and I allow them to tangle. My knee wedges between her thighs to press against her hot pussy.

She grinds down on a moan as I swallow down greedily. Her arousal fills the air as her juices coat my trouser leg. I flex my quads, and she groans at the added friction. Her humping becomes erratic as her orgasm barrels towards her.

I step back.

Her eyes fly open. Dazedly, she searches my face.

I shake my head.

"You disobeyed my command, *mate*," I tsk. "You will only cum when I tell you. *If* I tell you. And I'm inclined not to give you the release you crave."

"Jagger… *Please*," she cries, body shaking poised on the edge.

I ignore her plea and unhook her bra. Her delicious tits spill free from the cups as the front closure opens. I pinch both nipples, then rub them between my thumbs and index fingers as she pants through a slack mouth. My mouth returns to lave, suckle, and nip each one of her pebbled nipples until she's on the verge of another orgasm.

She throws her head back against the door and blows out a frustrated breath when I step back again.

"Jagger! Be fair! I had to do it my way," she cries, emerald green eyes plead for her release.

I move close to her again. My lips ghosts over hers, then trail lower—over her collarbone, between her tits, down her belly—to land on her laced-covered mons. A warm breath blown over her swollen slick pussy lips makes her shudder so hard, her shoulder blades bang against the door. A wicked chuckle puffs more air on her sensitive folds. She groans, eyes closed, head back.

A growl follows the ripping of the skimpy lingerie. It grows savage as I bury my face in her soaked pussy. My tongue pushes past the slick folds to lap every inch. Her thighs quiver on my shoulders as my fingers dig into her ass, locking her in place.

So intense, she still manages to buck as I devour her. My snarls join her cries. Her knees squeeze the sides of my head as her inner walls flutter. I increase my ministrations, tilting her pelvis to drive deeper into her core. A nip to her engorged clit, and she begs me to let her cum.

I jump to my feet, keeping her legs on my shoulders. Her body bent in half, I impale her on my thick cock. She screams as she cums all along my turgid length.

"You. Are. Mine. Sage. Waters. Mine!" I punctuate each word with a feral thrust. I continue to pound into her pussy as she climaxes again and again. "Do not disobey me ever again, Sage!"

I roar her name as my heavy balls draw up. One final thrust rocks me to the balls of my feet, thick thighs and firm ass flex. My cock spews copious amounts of seed inside of her womb. Once again, I pray for my seed to take root for my pup to fill my fated mate's belly.

Before my knees buckle from the ferocity of my release, I open the door. The silk belt slips from above the door. I close it and sag to the floor, twisting to put my ass down and Sage in my lap. She curls against my heaving chest with a sated sigh. I kiss the top of her head and let my eyes drift shut.

We can remain in blissed-out peace a moment longer and regain our strength before the meeting with her coven. The Fates know we'll need all our energy to face the next steps, including my pack.

CHAPTER 13

 agger

"What is the meaning of this nonsense?"

"Are the rumors true?"

"Is that even allowed?"

"Wow! A wolf shifter as our High Witch's fated mate?"

"I saw him and a bunch of other mongrels *strut inside of* our *coven led by Anala of all witches!"*

"And they're lurking around here like they own the place!"

"How did the Northeast Coven react to the news? What did Rupert say?!"

MY WOLF SENSES allow me to hear every spoken word members of Sage's coven utter despite me being in the room behind the High Witch's dais.

My wolf growls at each insult. An occasional remark by a member who sounds supportive brings me hope. Typically, the older witches complain while the younger ones appear more open. But with them being Immortal Witches, it's hard to distinguish who's of what age. Only their comments help to differentiate one group from the other.

I glance at Sage.

Showered and freshly dressed in an aqua blue suit with a pencil skirt and flesh-tone heels, she exudes power and beauty. She explained as an elemental witch of water, the colors of the ocean—the largest body of water—emphasize her connection to the element. My chest fills with pride to see her claiming bite uncovered. An unspoken acknowledgment to all our status as fated mates.

When we arrived ahead of the coven, she asked for space. Now, she sits on a chair with her eyes closed. A serene expression set on her lovely face as her mouth moves soundlessly.

My wolf and I stand not too far from her, keeping one eye on our fated mate and the other on the door leading to the coven's grand hall. Tag stands beside me while two of my men stand at the door leading to the hall and the one leading to Sage's private entry and the elevator for her family's residences. Several other enforcers cover areas throughout the floor and outside her penthouse duplex. Others remain on standby in vans outside of The Waters Tower. My wolf and I will protect my fated mate at all costs.

Even though Sage told me she heightened the level of protective wards around us, her sisters, and Anala—even though she's in New York. Sage's powers know no bounds.

However, the Alpha in me demands I have a hand in her safety. I also spoke with Garrett Moen—Alpha of the New York Wolves Pack—to not only monitor *Rupert*, but to watch Anala's back. Whatever may hurt my fated mate falls under my purview.

My gaze shifts to Willow and to Lillie across the room. That includes her younger sisters. I assigned enforcers as their security detail. Although they denied needing protection because of their powers, I insisted. Sage told them to just give in like she did with her new detail. They agreed for now. I chuckled to myself and thought forever, little ones.

Lillie senses my eyes on her and lifts her gaze to mine. She arches an elegant eyebrow. I shake my head and turn back to my fated mate.

She stirs, then her emerald green eyes open. They find my ice blue gaze on her, and a beatific smile spreads across her face, lighting her from within with a warm glow.

"It is time," Sage says as she rises. She pauses next to me

and angles her face for a kiss. I slant my mouth over hers and impart a kiss full of love, protection, and desire. When I step back, I catch Sage by the waist to steady her on wobbly legs. She grins at me. "Wow, thank you."

I smirk and brush my lips over hers as I rumble in my chest. Her eyes close on a sigh as her fingers tighten on my suit jacket—a new one she whipped up after our shower. And I can't wait for this meeting to end so I can have back in my arms. Alone in our home.

"Okay, lovebirds. Let's go, already."

Willow's comment with an exaggerated sigh, cuts into the bubble I share with my fated mate. I bite back a possessive growl.

Sage nods and smooths the front of my jacket, then pats my pecs with the corners of her lips curled up in a mischievous grin. Then she straightens her shoulders and walks with her head held high to the door leading to the coven's grand hall. Voices erupt as she enters.

My men and I are to wait until she calls me forward. The uproar of the crowd makes it difficult for me to heed my fated mate's request. A vicious growl rips from my chest. I pace behind the now closed door like a caged wild wolf separated from his fated mate—exactly what I am. Even it's only by a door. Tag and my men stand alert for any sounds of distress.

Sage's voice rings clear.

Sage

"I will have order. *Now*."

My emerald green eyes blaze as I pin several rambunctious members of the coven with a look of unbridled power. It surges over me and into the grand hall. Most of the vociferous ones have the respect to avert their eyes and bow their heads. I make note of them and of those who meet my gaze unfazed. However, all stop speaking at once and take their seats.

I wait until the entire room settles before I sit on the center chair reserved for the High Witch on the dais. Willow lowers to her seat on my right. The coven secretary sits at a table at my left to the side of the dais. Lillie sits in the first row opposite us, back straight, head held high like her sisters.

My eyes scan the crowd. Our parents did not join the meeting—at least not yet. I send a prayer to the Fates for Prudence and Wyatt to not cause any conflict. With a deep breath, I call the meeting to order.

"Good afternoon. It is 5:00, and I call the meeting of the Coven of the South to order."

The secretary calls each member's name from the coven roster and marks those present and those absent on her laptop. When she completes her task, she announces the number present. I'm not surprised to find all but a handful in attendance. I'm sure those gathered notice the obvious absence of my parents.

I shake it off and get to business.

"As you may now be aware, I called this meeting to inform you of my decision to cancel the pairing between Rupert Ravenheart of the Northeast Coven and me—"

Angry voices rise. I silence the room with a flick of my fingers, then continue.

"Last warning. Should anyone speak out of turn, I will eject you from this meeting," I state as my eyes rove over those in the grand hall. No one dares to open their mouth. "Whatever you may have heard, I will now tell you directly the events that led to this final decision."

I proceed to recount what happened ten years ago, ending with the return of my memories. A few murmured words of shock ripple through the members. They glance at one another in disbelief at my mother's actions. I assure them of the veracity of my words.

If it were not for Jagger being a wolf shifter, I am certain the coven would have agreed with me unanimously. However, after I open the floor to comments, those known to despise shifters—particularly wolves—rush to the two microphones.

I take a deep breath and brace myself before I recognize to speak a male witch around my mother's age.

"Sage, I must say how incredibly disappointed in you I am. We expected more from you as part of a long line of esteemed High Witches. And you've taken a wolf shifter as your mate," he says, lip curled in disgust. He glances around the room for a show of support. Several members nod and murmur their agreement. He turns back to me.

"And where is this *mate* of yours? Hiding behind your skirt?"

A ferocious growl rips through the air as the door to the Hight Witch's chamber bursts open, nearly tearing from its hinges. The grand hall erupts in shouts and screams as Jagger—followed by Tag and the security team—enter the space.

I jump to my feet and stare at Jagger, silently begging him to control himself and his wolf. Now is not the time to lose it. His flashing eyes land on me, and he stalks forward. He stops with his body angled between the rest of the grand hall and me. His chest heaves with the exertion to hold his wolf at bay.

"And *this* is what you expect us to accept, Sage?"

The witch's snicker causes Jagger to flex his fingers. I place a hand on his back. His muscles taut with beneath my palm. Through our connection, I sense his anger. It burns and threatens to upend the grand hall—the world, if need be—to protect me.

I step from behind him and face the witch.

"You know not the depth of a fated mate, Cyrus. So, no, I do not expect you to accept the bond Jagger and I share necessarily. But you will respect it and him. Do not belittle your status in the coven for petty displays."

Cyrus bristles as I recognize the next speaker. He opens his mouth to protest. But I silence him with a stare. He moves aside and returns to his seat. Those around him lean in to whisper. I make note of them too.

The speakers continue with those against and those in

support of Jagger and me. Others voice their concerns about offending the Northeast coven. After more than an hour, I call for the last speakers. No one steps to the microphones.

"The meeting stands adjourned. The time is 6:30," I say, keeping my voice firm and clear, then rise from the chair.

Jagger and his men who stood the entire time behind me follow me towards the smaller room. Tag steps forward to enter it ahead of me. He scans the space, then nods it's clear for us to enter. Willow and Lillie join us.

"Fuck—"

I raise my finger to my lips and shake my head at Jagger, then gesture for us to continue to the private elevator. Once the doors close, I take a deep breath. Jagger rages, all but yanking on his white blond hair. I don't interrupt him.

We step off to my entry foyer. The enforcers at the double doors stand aside to give us access. Jagger tells them to remain alert while Tag speaks to the ones stationed around The Tower.

"I find it unnerving Mother and Father didn't show. What do you make of it, Sage?" Lillie asks as we sit in the living room.

A ragged sigh slips past my lips as I slump back against the silk sofa. Jagger stops his pacing and sits beside me. His arm goes around my shoulders, and he pulls me into his side. I close my eyes as he nuzzles my hair. His rumbling soothes me.

Reluctantly, I sit up. We'll have time later to cuddle... I hope. A shudder runs through me at the thought of not being with Jagger. But judging by the reaction of the coven, I can't say for certain how things will end up. I pat Jagger's muscular thigh when he sits up and stares at me questioningly.

"They must stand firm in their beliefs still. I have not heard from either of them. So, your guess is as good as mine. I would hope they won't incite any conflict," I respond. "However, I was pleased to see so many members offer their support. This comes as a shock. I'll give the coven time to absorb the news, then meet again."

I glance over at Willow, where she stands by the wall of windows overlooking Biscayne Bay and the Atlantic Ocean beyond. Her shoulders hunch around her ears as tension emanates from her. I stand and go to my younger sister.

Jagger cocks an eyebrow. But I shake my head and walk to Willow.

"Hey, Willow. What are your thoughts?" I ask quietly as I slide the door open to the wraparound terrace.

She hesitates, then follows me outside. We stop at the glass divider and lean on the railing. I wait for her to answer.

Willow shrugs.

"I have to admit some of their points are valid, Sage. Especially the lineage of the next High Witch, your daughter," she starts, then casts a sidelong glance at me. I keep my face expressionless, not wanting to discourage her from speaking unhindered. She takes a deep breath and continues. "I love you and want what's best for you. But the coven can't remain strong if it's divided. Then there's the Witch Council to consider."

Willow stops and takes a deep breath as her eyes continue to stare out to the ocean.

I hold my tongue.

"But you're right. The news comes as a shock. Once members have time to think on it—given you provided the full story—they may change their minds. It's a matter of waiting, I suppose," she says, then pushes off the railing. "It's been a long day. I want to soak in a tub with lavender essential oil and a glass of Cabernet Sauvignon. Do you mind if I call it a night?"

I mimic her move and stand as I shake my head.

"Of course not," I respond and put my arms around her for a hug. "Thank you, Willow, for your honesty. Never think you cannot come to me, no matter what you think my reaction may be. Above all, you are my sister, my blood. Do you understand?"

I pull back to search her face. She lowers her eyes. But raises them to meet my gaze and nods.

"Aaw! Sister's group hug!"

Lillie's arms fling around us.

"Boy! What a day, huh? Time for a bath and wine. Heck, maybe even the entire bottle!" She says with a light laugh as she loops her arms through ours and leads us back inside.

I walk them to the elevator, not reacting to Jagger's raised eyebrow as we pass him. Once in the entry foyer, I give my sisters another hug and bid them goodnight. When the elevator doors close, Willow meets my gaze with forlorn eyes. A shiver runs through me, and I wrap my arms around my waist.

Muscular arms cover mine as a firm chest presses into my back. I sigh and lean into my fated mate. His strength washes over me as his rumbles soothe the sorrow in my soul. I close my eyes and pray to the Fates Willow will not turn against me too.

"Let's go home, beautiful mate of mine."

Jagger's huskily spoken words save me from the moment of despair.

I nod my head in agreement as my heart constricts. At this moment, with my parents and now potentially my sister in opposition to me and my fated mate, this does not feel like home anymore.

CHAPTER 14

 *agger*

"WHAT IS THIS? The Wolf, the Witch, and the Wardrobe? You have more clothes than me! Where will I put mine?"

My fated mate's questions followed by giggles float from within my dressing room.

It's nice to hear a light air from Sage. Since last night, she's been sad and doubting herself. But I keep telling her she's a badass and those in her coven who oppose us can fuck off.

After the meeting, she used her teleportation magick to bring us, Tag, and my enforcers within The Tower to my mansion on Moon Island. The others drove back in the vans. She didn't want a skirmish as we left through the

135

lobby. I agreed because they would not hold me responsible for my wolf tearing through some witches if they threatened my fated mate or my pack.

Once my enforcers pledged to stand by my side, they left Viggo, Tag, and me to discuss the next steps, including a pack meeting. They were no more thrilled than I was with the outcome of the witches' meeting. Tag voiced his concerns of the pack accepting Sage, standing with me should the witches retaliate, and whether someone may challenge me as Alpha.

His last concern made my wolf bristle—ears flattened to his skull, canines bared. A savage growl issued in warning. My lip curled as I snapped out a reminder, I will finish anyone who dares to challenge me. No one will keep me from my fated mate. No. One.

But I will give up all to keep Sage by my side.

I wonder if she will do the same.

"Seriously, Jagger. You're not a wolf shifter, you're a clothes horse!"

Sage's snorts as she doubles over in a fit of giggles washes away the negative thought. She leans against the doorframe and wipes tears from the corners of her eyes. My silk robe swallows her petite body. Then she pauses as the disquiet in my mind passes along our mating bond.

Each day, it gets stronger. Our feelings transmitted along the tether that binds us as a mated pair.

She rubs her chest as her eyes scan my face.

I won't let my unwarranted doubt worry my fated mate. So, I stalk towards her until her butt hits a wall and her mouth opens in a perfect O, then cage her between my forearms.

"A horse, huh? Is my cock not large enough for you, *mate*?" I ask, our noses inches apart.

Lust explodes within her emerald green eyes as a breath escapes her open mouth. She blinks and shakes her head.

"Oh, no, you won't flip my words, Jagger Larson. I said nothing about your dick. Only the amount of clothes you have and no room for mine," she replies.

I chuckle and brush my lips over hers. She melts against me. But I stand and take her hand.

"You missed something, *mate*."

Sage gasps when I open a door on the other side of the bedroom. Her eyes dart around the space as she takes in the all-white Carrara marble bathroom. A walk-in Roman shower big enough to hold four, an extra-large silver wolf-claw-foot tub, a single vanity with an adjacent makeup table, and a separate water closet for the bidet and toilet.

I usher her inside and towards another door.

Her eyes shine as she scans the dressing room. A hand-carved white island with a white suede top and drawers sits in the center. Three walls accommodate racks and drawers for clothing. Shelves for handbags and shoes flank the door. In one corner, a trifold mirror surrounds a raised platform.

Sage steps forward and skims her fingers over the designer day dresses, skirt suits, blouses, and evening gowns. She opens drawers and smirks at the Agent Provocateur lingerie and playsuits laid out on silk liners. When she turns to face me, her mouth drops open at the dazzling array of Hermès Birkin bags—red Togo leather, matte black alligator, the impossible to get Himalayan with diamond details. She steps forward, entranced.

Now, I smirk.

"Satisfied, *mate*?"

"Jagger! Why didn't you show me last night? When did you do all of this? And you bought the correct sizes!" She exclaims as she throws her arms around my neck, wiggling her curvy little body all over me as she dances on her toes. "Thank you! Thank you!"

"I believe we had other things on our minds…"

I cup her ass, lifting her to grind my burgeoning erection—hung, but not horse size—against her pussy mound. My mouth catches hers as she plants a kiss on my cheek. A nip followed by a lick has her wiggling for other reasons.

"You like?" I say gruffly in her ear as I thrust my hips upwards, holding her down against my cock. I respond to her mewl with a wicked chuckle. "Let's see how much."

I stride towards the center island and sit my fated mate on top with her ass cheeks on the edge. When I press my palm between her tits, she leans back on her elbows. Hooded eyes stare up at me. They follow as I lower my face between her welcoming thighs. We maintain eye contact as I swipe the sides of my silk robe away from my reward.

The calloused pads of my thumbs drag along the edges of her bare mons. The delicate flesh quivers in their wake. So responsive, her pussy lips begin to glisten with her juices. My nose twitches, full of her instant arousal. I groan, hungry for the succulent taste of her.

My thumbs pull her lower lips apart to expose her slick core. I stare at it transfixed, as it winks and weeps for me.

"Jagger… I need you…"

"Hush, baby, I know what you need and when you need it."

Sage whines as her head falls back, eyes squeezed shut. My hand snakes out, fingers curl around her throat. Her eyes pop open.

"Eyes on me," I command as I tighten my grip. Her breath catches as I continue. "I want to watch you break for me."

Her pupils dilate.

Moisture coats my other thumb. I glance down to find her pussy gushed at my words. I lean down and purr as I lap at her sweet juices. My eyes never leave hers as my tongue swirls to capture every single drop.

"Unnhhh… Jagger. Oh, right there. Oh!" My fated mate's cries of carnal passion urge me to probe deeper with slow, long licks. A few well-placed nips add a bite of pain to her pleasure. She writhes and moans louder. Her eyes remain locked with mine.

However, my eyes want to roll to the back of my head in pure ecstasy. Her taste and arousal so divine, I can barely contain myself—or my wolf. The tip and several thick inches of my cock poke from the waistband of my joggers. I feel pre-cum collecting on its mushroom tip. My cock wants in on the action.

Who am I to deny it?

But I'll wait. I want my fated mate soft and dripping for me before I mount her from behind. With a groan, I add my fingers to the mix. One, then two drill into her pussy while my tongue wraps around her distended clit.

"Jagger! I… I can—can't hold back," my fated mate cries anxiously as her wide eyes plead with me.

I blow a puff of air over her slick folds before I respond, "Cum for me, my beautiful mate. Cum for me now!"

She screams as my teeth nip her clit and my fingers spear her pussy. The knuckles graze her G-spot. Her eyes flutter closed as her body convulses and her pussy clamps on my digits. She writhes as I lap at the flood of juices. I press my palm above her mons to make her still so she can focus on the pleasure rippling through her body. Her screams turn into a baby howl.

I spring to my feet as I yank the tie on my joggers. My aching cock bounces out. I grip its base and plunge my length into her quivering pussy. She's so tight as her pussy clenches, it takes effort to fit all of me inside of her. I feed it to her inch by agonizing inch. My wolf snarls. He wants all in. Now.

My fingers strum her clit to keep her orgasm on high until I'm fully seated. Her pussy continues to flutter around my length as I thrust with wild abandon. I want to pound the worry and fear from her body. Hell, from mine too. All that matters is we are one. Whole. Never apart again.

Her cries and moans please my wolf. We make it our mission to bring absolute pleasure to our fated mate. My hips circle as I change the angle to drive deeper. I pull out and flip her around with a few smacks to her round ass before I plow back into her. My torso presses hers into the center island. Her hips held aloft by my tight grip grind into the edge with each brutal thrust.

"MINE! Dammit! MINE!" I roar.

My fated mate shudders at my frenetic outburst, even as her pussy clamps on my cock. We groan in unison. I keep pumping, intent on finding my release. My knees shake as the first zap of erotic energy hits my lower spine. It zings to my balls and out to the tip of my pulsating cock. It thickens more than possible. With a savage roar, ropes of my seed shoot into her womb.

"You. Are. Mine, Sage. Waters. MINE!"

I bury my face in the side of her sweat dampened neck. My cock pushed to the maximum inside of her pussy. She babbles an incoherent response as her fingers twine with mine on either side of her head. Our pants mingle. Heartbeats race.

We remain locked as one until I step back and watch as my cock slides from her well-used pussy. She groans louder than me with longing for more. I tap her pussy lips and smirk as my seed dribbles from her core down the curve of her ass. I scoop up some on a finger and press it to her slack mouth. Her little pink tongue darts out to lap the digit clean. I groan as my cock twitches, ready to go again.

Alas, we cannot. Duty calls.

I slip the robe from my fated mate and scoop her into my arms. As I carry her to the Roman shower, she nuzzles against my chest with a contented sigh. I wish we could stay at home in bed. But we have the pack meeting to attend in an hour.

Her plump brown nipples tighten as I bathe them with a soapy sponge. I'm torn between suckling them and getting her washed and dressed. Instead, I take a deep breath, then groan when her arousal fills my nose. I shake my head and re-focus on my task.

"Jagger, I can do it," Sage says as she reaches for the sponge. "How much time do we have? We can't be late."

Even in her post-coital haze, my fated mate's concern is for us. I lean over and brush my lips against hers as I assure her we have plenty of time. She gives in with a sigh and leans against the marble wall.

Quickly, I wash her, then myself. She protests when I carry her from the shower. But I ignore her and dry her soft skin with a heated towel. Sage makes her way to her dressing room. I swat her ass just to fuck with her. She covers it with one hand as she scowls at me over her shoulder. Hips sway to a natural rhythm as she walks away.

I leave her bathroom for my dressing room. When I reemerge, Sage stands by the window dressed in a three-quarter sleeve, navy blue dress that accentuates her curves and falls below her knees. The boat neck reveals my claiming bite. Strappy sandals lengthen her toned legs and give her ass an added boost. Her ebony curls flow down her back. She turns as I enter the bedroom.

"Don't you look dapper, my Alpha," my fated mates says

as her appreciative eyes scan me from head to toe in my custom Brioni suit.

My heart soars at her possessive use of my title. I grin and respond huskily, "As do you, my Luna."

I extend my arm, and she loops hers through it. In the entry, Viggo, Tag, Rust, Karl, and my security detail wait for us. I pause to introduce Sage to my younger brother before we leave the mansion.

Calls to my youngest sibling, Signy, went to her voicemail. I haven't had time to question my sister. My hope is we'll speak after the pack meeting. Unless, of course, she's sided with our parents. I shake my head to clear the negative thought and stride towards the front doors.

Instead of golf carts, Suburbans wait to take us to the clubhouse. I agreed with Tag it's best to have the protection of an entire SUV and not the openness of the golf cart. I lift Sage onto the back seat, then circle around to the other side. She takes my hand as I sit beside her. Tag drives and Viggo rides in the passenger seat.

It's quiet as we ride to the center of Moon Island. The clubhouse appears as the lane opens up. The two-story structure accommodates our meeting space, recreation rooms, and a grill that serves burgers, fries, shakes, and other backyard-style food.

A few golf carts and cars sit in the parking area. Most members walked from their homes.

Viggo nudges me as I reach to open Sage's door. He inclines his head towards the side of the clubhouse. I follow his gaze.

Melissa struts towards us. Her amber eyes locked on me.

I mutter a curse under my breath. I've ignored her calls and text messages ever since her unexpected appearance in my suite at Club Sol & Mani. It didn't occur to me she would find a pack meeting as the time to approach me. Fuck.

Distracted, my hand hovers over the door handle. A moment later, the door bumps into me as it opens from the inside, just as Melissa reaches me.

"Jagger, why haven't you answered my calls and texts?" She demands, lips formed in a pout. "Do you want me to grovel or what?"

Sage's body brushes against my back as she slides from the SUV.

I don't even have to turn around to see her face to gauge her reaction. Her surprise comes through our tether, loud and clear. I send back reassurance in hopes to diffuse the situation.

"Who the hell is *she?*" Melissa snarls. Her amber eyes flash with streaks of gold as she glares at Sage. "Oh, so is *she* the reason you stopped fucking me, Jagger?"

My fated mate stiffens beside me.

"Now is not the time, Melissa. Go into the clubhouse," I command.

When she hesitates with her wolf hovering at the surface, glaring at Sage, I issue a warning growl. The sable-haired hellion jumps. She walks backwards, keeping her narrowed eyes on Sage.

Other pack members take notice and pause before entering the clubhouse to watch the exchange with interest. Tag steps forward and gestures for them to go inside. Their curious gazes flick between Melissa's retreating figure and me. A few cock their heads at the sight of Sage, noses lifted as they scent the air.

I put my arm around her waist and pull her against my side.

"Don't worry. What the she-wolf said is not true. I will explain later," I murmur in her ear. I keep my voice low to avoid others hearing us with the enhanced reach of wolf sifter ears. When Sage nods, I relax.

We enter the clubhouse and head for the meeting space. It accommodates our entire pack, set up with tiered seating and two aisles that lead to the raised platform. Already filled, Sage, Viggo, Tag, Rust, Karl, and I stride down one aisle while my enforcers line the walls. I bring Sage onto the dais with me. She sits in the chair reserved for the Luna. I had it placed there from storage earlier. She crosses her legs and smooths her dress over her thighs before she lifts her head with her back straight and stares out at our pack.

Murmurs arise. Members shift in their seats to get a better view of the female who sits beside me as my mate. I raise my hand to call for silence.

"That's Sage Waters! She's the High Witch!" Melissa's angry snarl reverberates around the space just before she shifts into her wolf and leaps towards the dais.

Then all hell breaks loose.

CHAPTER 15

Sage

"Viggo, Karl, get my fated mate out of here. Now!"

Karl grabs my arm. The huge wolf shifter lifts me to my feet with ease.

However, my eyes never leave the she-wolf named Melissa. Her sable-haired wolf races towards me with ears flat and snapping jaws. Around her, others shift into their wolves or rush to their feet. Shouts blend with the sound of ripping clothing and claws scrapping the stone floor.

In my periphery, Jagger tears through his suit like tissue paper as his great silvery white wolf charges forth with a blood-curdling howl and canines bared. On his other side, Tag's massive brown wolf paws the floor with his ears flattened to his head. Rust's huge red wolf snarls and snaps his jaws. Standing between me and the mad she-wolf, Viggo morphs into a giant red wolf. His ice blue eyes flash silvery, and his lips curl in a snarl as he takes a defensive stance.

My lips move on instinct.

Melissa yowls when her wolf slams into the invisible barrier I erected around the dais. She bounces back as her limbs flail to gain purchase on the stone. When she rights herself, her amber eyes shoot venomous daggers at me. Blood pours from her muzzle. She paces along the barrier snarling as she attempts to find a weakness.

There is never a weakness in my magick. She should know since she outed me as High Witch. I watch her dispassionately.

The space falls quiet as others stop and stare at me. Karl's grip on my arm lessens until I extricate it from him gently. I move to Jagger's side. His wolf stares up at me. Through our tether, he sends his love and admiration. I return it tenfold.

My fated mate would risk himself and his pack to save me. With no uncertainty, I now realize I will do the same for him. If the coven decides against our mating, then I will walk away with my head held high and Jagger by my side.

I smile at him, then turn to sit in my chair.

JAGGER

. . .

I WATCH my fated mate settle back on her Luna's chair—a position she just cemented with one simple move. She meets my gaze and bows her head in a sign of respect for my role as Alpha. I grin as best as I can in wolf form—more sharp teeth than curved lips.

Then I swing my head around to face my pack. My parents don't appear amongst those gathered, nor Signy. Despite my disappointment, I don't let it impede my control over my pack. I eye each member until they lower their heads in submission. All but a few—including the sable-haired hellion who started the ruckus—return my stare as wolves and in human form. I throw my head back and howl. It bounces off the walls around the room. I continue until members join in.

Our song continues a moment longer, then I command my wolf to recede. He does so reluctantly, not wanting to leave our fated mate. I assure him she will be more than fine. When I stand on two feet, I notice some members followed my lead and shifted. I eye those who remain in wolf form.

"Shift. Now!" I bellow, drawing on the force of my Alpha command.

Some do so immediately. Still others hesitate. Their eyes filled with hostility focus on my fated mate. I issue a warning growl, and they sift. But once again, Melissa defies me.

I glance at Sage over my shoulder. She nods and releases her barrier spell. I stalk towards Melissa. Tag and Rust stride beside me while Viggo and Karl stand by my fated mate. When I reach Melissa, I grab her wolf by the scruff.

"Shift. Right. Now!" I command with a rough shake for each word.

She hisses and snaps her jaws.

"Last warning, Melissa," I say in a deep voice that brokers no disobedience.

Still held by the neck, she releases her wolf, then glowers at me.

"She's a *witch*! Look at how she hurt me with her *magick*!" Melissa whines as she rubs her nose. Blood trickles from it. But already her enhanced healing ability repairs the damage from her face-plant into Sage's invisible barrier. Melissa's face reddens more from embarrassment than from harm.

"Serves you right!"

A she-wolf who Melissa enjoys bullying shouts from her seat.

"Yeah! You finally met your match this time, Melissa!"

Another she-wolf yells from the back row.

The space fills with more voices—those for and those against. I release Melissa and raise my hand for silence. At once, everyone stills. Meanwhile, her anger and jealousy roll off her in waves.

"Those who shifted go to your lockers and dress, then return so we can begin the meeting properly. Five minutes," I pronounce. Without a glance at Melissa, I pivot on my heel and stalk towards my fated mate. Viggo and Karl give me nods as they move from Sage's side to enter the room behind the dais for clothes. Tag and Rust wait for me.

"I apologize we're not as well behaved as your witches," I say as I crouch in front of her, ashamed by my pack's outburst. She shakes her head. My hands slide up her legs, needing to feel her. "Baby, are you all right?" I ask

She smiles, and responds, "Yes, my Alpha. Thank you for protecting me."

I rumble in my chest. She bites the corner of her lip, then widens her eyes at my erection standing tall between us. I shrug with a smirk, accustomed to being naked and aroused after a shift.

"Oh, no! No one sees my mate's stuff!" Sage declares. A microsecond later, I'm fully clothed in a fresh version of my suit. "Hunh. Much better."

I chuckle and stand, brushing my lips over hers.

"Thank you, my love," I murmur against her lips. My heart skips a beat at the word love.

Sage smirks and says, "You can thank me properly later. But first, duty calls."

I turn and survey the space. Everyone who shifted returned clothed and sit waiting for the meeting to begin, including Melissa. A hush descends as I scan the room. I take my seat.

"Now, the meeting begins. Any further disruptions will lead to that member being banned from the meeting and dealt with as I deem necessary," I say, as my eyes land on Melissa. She flares her nostrils but remains quiet. "I called this meeting to inform you of my fated mate."

Murmurs arise again. More subdued this time. But I will allow no interruptions.

"Need I remind you to remain silent until called upon?" I ask in a low, deadly voice. I wait until I hear not a sound. "Many of you know my strong desire to mate with only the female the Fates chose for me. Ten years ago, I was in the Everglades…"

By the time I complete the recap of our story, the entire room sits in stunned silence. I allow them time to digest this information. Most of them flick their gazes to study Sage. She sits like a queen on her throne. Poised and regal with an open expression to offer trust and serenity to our pack.

"Alpha, may I speak?"

I look towards the center of the meeting space. An elder wolf shifter stands, awaiting my approval to speak. I've known him since I was a little pup, and he's always been kind to me. He's of an indeterminate age, having been around since my grandfather was Alpha. Bo earns the respect of the pack for his wise council and unbiased opinions. I'm eager to hear his reaction to my news.

"Yes, Bo, come forward and say your piece," I respond.

He walks to stand before the dais. His eyes move from me to Sage. He inclines his gray head at her.

"Luna, I know your people, your grandmother, in fact. She was a wise witch who understood the importance of respect amongst paranormal beings. You remind me of her, even in the short time I've seen you. You have grace and control. Knowing how powerful your grandmother was, you could have easily destroyed our pack with a flick of your fingers. You did not. Instead, you controlled the situation, then stepped back for our Alpha to perform his duties."

Bo turns to face the rest of the pack as he continues.

"And perform his duties, Alpha Jagger Larson shall, as he has all these years. It is not as uncommon as you may think for a wolf shifter and a witch to mate, particularly with fated mates. I support our Alpha and our Luna. May the Fates bless them with many strong pups."

Bo faces Sage and me again and bows his head before he returns to his seat.

Rumblings begin, and I issue a warning growl. The room falls silent again.

More pack members come forward to speak. All remain respectful. The most vehement concern is for the Alpha's bloodline. What happens if our offspring can't shift? How can a witch lead a pack of wolf shifters? What if they don't want to stay with the pack and choose the coven? Fortunately, not one challenges me as Alpha. Then Melissa asks to speak. Not having a choice, I allow her request.

She makes a show of approaching the dais. Her lithe figure outlined in a gossamer slip of a dress. At one time, the sight of Melissa would have awakened my cock. Now, it lies flaccid against my thigh. The only pussy it wants is my fated mate's delicious core.

Melissa tosses her waist-long sable mane when she stops before me. She licks her lips seductively.

"My Alpha--"

Through the tether, I feel Sage's irritation at Melissa's innuendo. I send back reassurance and love to settle my fated mate.

"—please accept my most humble apology for my behavior," Melissa starts and pauses for my recognition. I give a grunt. A brilliant smile spreads across her face as though I proposed marriage to her. Then she continues. "The appearance of another female surprised me, given the fact you and I were intimate for years—"

My growl cuts her off. She blinks, glancing around, feigning innocence.

"I... I mean you and I mated many, many, many times—"

"Melissa, do not attempt to make more of the fucking than what it was. I made myself very clear to you it was to satisfy a need, no more than food or water does for the body. You agreed and 'mated many, many, many times' with many, many, many other males in this pack and in others. Correct?"

I raise my gaze to those gathered.

More than a few males voice their agreement. I glance back at Melissa. Her face contorts as her wolf battles to come forth. I cock a warning eyebrow at her as Tag growls. Her nostrils flare.

"Whatever, *Alpha*! However, I issue a challenge to the witch," Melissa spits out, teeth bared.

Gasps ring around the space. Even I'm shocked. I feel Viggo, Tag, Rust, and Karl glance at me.

"*My* Alpha, may I speak?"

My head swivels on my neck so quickly, the room spins. I stare at Sage as I push across the tether, begging her to let me handle Melissa. My fated mate ignores my pleas as she sits forward and meets my shocked gaze with her determined one. I nod, unable to verbalize a response. Sage hasn't even shifted yet. Unless she's allowed to use her magick, how can she beat the pugnacious she-wolf? The challenging pair makes the rules, not the Alpha.

Fuck!

Sage shifts her gaze to Melissa.

"I do not know you or the situation you had with my fated mate. However, I can understand your desire to keep him. Jagger Larson is a wolf shifter any female would be proud to call her mate—in the bed and out of it. To that I can attest to many, many, many, *many* times."

Snickers from the room make Melissa's face flame crimson as Sage turns the sable-haired hellion's words on her.

"I accept your challenge"—my fated mate holds up a finger when Melissa speaks—"on one condition. You will abide by whatever decision the pack Alpha decides afterwards. Agreed?"

Melissa's eyes narrow as she considers Sage's words.

"Agreed. However, you cannot use your witch's magick!" Melissa declares as she folds her arms under her breasts and smirks in triumph.

I sit forward. But Sage speaks.

"Agreed, as long as you do not shift. We meet female to female, barehanded."

The smirk slides from Melissa's face, then she shrugs. "Fine, *witch*! I don't need my wolf to beat you."

Sage nods her head and rises from her seat. I jump to my feet. But she lays a hand on my forearm and smiles up at me. Love floods across our tether. My wolf snarls as he paces. I pull on every source of my control to stop myself from snatching my fated mate and racing from the club-house straight to our mansion. Hell! Straight to *Moonbeam*, so we can sail away.

The pack moves outdoors to the patch of grass reserved for situations such as this one. However, females rarely step onto the grass in a challenge. I scowl as I take Sage's hand and follow.

Melissa stands in the middle of the patch buck naked.

Sage ignores her display. In an instant, her navy blue dress changes to a catsuit and her curls form a tight bun on top of her head. Barefoot, she steps on the grass.

I join them in the middle and have them agree once more to the challenge and terms. Neither one hesitates. I tell them the challenge lasts until one of them yields to the other. Females may not fight to the death. They're too valuable to the future of a pack. The Alpha decides if the loser remains or sends them to another pack. When my last plea down our tether goes ignored, I step off the patch.

With a feral growl, Melissa charges arms outstretched, and long fingernails directed at Sage. A second before contact, she steps aside. Melissa barrels forward and bumps into a she-wolf, who pushes her back onto the patch as she shouts for the bully to take her beating.

Wild-eyed, Melissa glances around for Sage. Another attempted charge fails. The grace with which Sage leaps aside or pivots draws praise from the pack. However, she remains focused on Melissa. The next time she rushes at Sage, instead of stepping aside, she spins and drops to the ground with a scissor kick. The move knocks Melissa's legs from beneath her. Sage pounces onto Melissa's back and pins her arms to her sides. She flails, but Sage holds firm.

"Enough! Yield, Melissa. Now!" my fated mate commands as she holds strong to the sable-haired hellion.

Melissa screeches as her body bucks to toss Sage from her back. Realizing the gig is up, Melissa mutters yield.

Sage leaps backwards to land in a crouch, then stands a distance from Melissa and next to me. My fated mate smiles up at me and winks. I wrap my arms around her, lift her from the ground, and bury my face against her neck.

The pack breaks out in raucous shouts, stomping feet, and wolf whistles. The voices of every single one of the she-wolves and some males Melissa subjected to her bouts of bullying rise higher than the rest. Someone begins the chant of 'Luna' and others pick it up.

Melissa stands and faces us with her head bowed awaiting my judgement.

I look at my fated mate. She puts her hand on my chest and murmurs the decision is for me to make. I turn to Melissa.

"Melissa, what do you have to say for yourself?"
Surprisingly, she doesn't puff up or yell.

"I apologize, Luna, Alpha. I promise to behave and hope you will not force me from the pack," she mumbles.

I consider her words, then respond.

"Apology accepted, Melissa. As Alpha, I never want to lose a member of my pack. However, if necessary, I will transfer the offending member to another pack if they will take them."

Melissa shudders, a small cry escapes from her mouth.

"This is not your first offense. But I will grant you the opportunity to prove you will be a peaceful member of the Miami Wolves Pack over the next few months"—her head snaps up with wide eyes—"Should you stray to your old ways, you will no longer be welcome amongst us. Do you understand?"

Her mouth opens and closes as her gaze darts between my fated mate and me. Sage maintains an impassive face. Melissa looks at me and nods.

"Yes, Alpha, I understand. Thank you, Alpha," she responds gratefully.

I nod, then lift my gaze to my pack.

"Does anyone else take issue with Sage Waters as my fated mate or me as your Alpha?" My eyes rove over the crowd.

Many speak up to support our pairing. Others don't hold my gaze. I make note of them. Then announce the meeting is over. I swoop my fated mate into my arms and stride towards the Suburbans. Viggo, Tag, Rust, Karl, and the enforcers follow us.

Once inside the SUV with Sage on my lap, I ask her how she learned her defensive moves.

"I train with a witch who's a world champion MMA fighter," she replies with a shrug. "I have to defend myself with more than my magick."

I chuckle, then hope it won't be necessary for her to defend herself at all as my thoughts return to those who oppose our pairing—witches and wolves.

CHAPTER 16

 *agger*

"You disobey me, mate. I do not agree with your return to The Waters Tower. And damn sure not without me!"

Sage jumps when my bellow rises to the ceiling as we stand in the living room of our Moon Island mansion. But she recovers and folds her arms beneath her lush tits as her eyes narrow on me.

We're deadlocked in our first argument. She insists she must return to normal activities to avoid giving the witches any reason to complain about her, or worse. I don't trust those fuckers and want to keep her close and safe here on Moon Island. With me!

"You see! You see! That's why I told you we couldn't

work! We have responsibilities—you to your pack and me to my coven and all witches. How can I do my role when you want to confine me to your side?! Yet you can go about your duties uninterrupted."

Sage throws her hands in the air as her temper matches mine in intensity.

I stumble back at the force of her words as much as their meaning. How could she go back to her past doubts at this point? We're bonded dammit! She bears my claiming bite. The only part left is our mate bonding ceremony and wedding, if she wishes.

No! I refuse to let her backtrack on us.

I stalk towards her. She stands her ground with hands on her hips and emerald green eyes blazing. They waver as the sound of my deep-chested rumbling reaches her ears and the unconditional love I send through our tether caresses her heart. By the time I reach her, she melts into my embrace.

One arm bands around her waist, holding her close to my chest while the other hand strokes her back. My lips brush across the top of her silky curls as I murmur words of love to my fated mate. She trembles and tightens her grip on my back.

"I'm scared, Jagger. I just don't know what they'll do—"

My protective growl cuts her off. But she shakes her head and continues.

"No, I don't mean as in harm me. Rather, they demand I step down as the leader of the coven, High Witch, and head of the Witch Council. I don't know what I would do! Aside from my jewelry making, my entire life centered on training for the roles. I never imagined a different one. Well, not until you."

Sage lifts her face to stare up into my eyes.

"You changed everything, Jagger Larson. The course of a life pre-planned for me by my mother from the moment she conceived me. I love you. And if it means I lose my coven to keep you, then I will. But I have to try and make both work. So, I must go to The Tower with my head held high and your claiming bite and ring on my finger. I hope you understand, Jagger."

She ends with tears spilling down her flushed cheeks.

With a ragged cry, I crush my mouth to hers. My tongue pushes past her quivering lips to possess her. I want to drive away her fears and replace them with our love and our combined strength. Together, we can surpass any challenge. I pour every ounce of my passion into the earnest kiss.

"Fuck, baby. I love you so much it hurts! Never fear. We stand together as one. Okay?"

Cupping her beautiful face in my sizable hands, I speak the words as I kiss the tears away from her cheeks. She sobs but nods. Watery eyes stare up at mine, shining bright with uninhibited emotion.

"I have to go, Jagger," Sage whispers.

"I know you do, baby. But first"—I scoop her into my arms and head for the stairs—"I'm going to show you just how much I love you, my fated mate."

The corners of her lips curl up slowly. I bend my head

and kiss her again, then bound up the stairs three at a time. And my scent will cover her to warn every single one of those male fuckers to back the hell up.

"WHAT HAVE YOU HEARD FROM SIGNY?"

At my question, Viggo averts his ice blue eyes—so like mine and our father's. Then reaches up and pulls his red, shoulder-length hair into a ponytail. Pack tattoos on the buzzed sides of his head stand out in contrast to the pale skin. He uses the move to bide himself some time.

Great. So, it can't be good. Hopefully, Signy meets us for a run in the Everglades, as I requested. While Sage goes to The Tower—with Njal, the head of her security detail, and three others after I instituted my Alpha command—I want to connect with my siblings. Get them away from the rest of our pack, particularly from our parents.

Viggo re-affirmed his allegiance to me.

Signy? No word.

As I turn from my Sikorsky S-92 Executive Helicopter to get back in the golf cart and ride to my mansion, I see Signy driving towards us. Her waist-length ebony hair pulled into a ponytail flies behind her like a banner as the wind whips past the open top of her white-on-red Porsche 911 Carrera Turbo Cabriolet. She parks next to my golf cart and hops from her supercar. Shield sunglasses block her ice blue eyes, so I can't gauge her mood.

Instead, I watch her body language as she struts

towards Viggo and me. At five feet, nine inches, her long, toned legs eat up the distance between us. She moves with predatory grace and power, unwavering. When she stands before me, she bows her head in a show of respect.

"Alpha, I apologize for being late. A mechanic had to change the tire—"

"Yeah, because you drive too damn fast!" Viggo cuts in with a frown on his handsome face.

Signy takes her sunglasses off and gives him a scathing look. Then she turns back to me.

"Anyway… Here I am. As commanded," she says.

I bite back a retort. She came. So, that's a good sign.

"Let's go," I say instead and gesture towards the helicopter.

The pilot steps aboard while the flight attendant stays beside the aircraft. She climbs in after us and closes the door.

"Would you care for a beverage or a snack, Alpha?" The she-wolf asks. When I decline, she asks my siblings. Viggo winks at her and nods. Signy rolls her eyes at our brother's flirtatious behavior and declines. The flight attendant disappears through the door leading to the galley and cockpit.

I settle back in the plush leather chair and pull out my mobile to check for a text message from my fated mate. Finding none, I send one to check in. I grin as she responds she's fine since Njal—the Giant—shadows her everywhere she goes.

A cough interrupts my response.

I glance up to find Signy staring at me with pursed lips. I cock an eyebrow in question.

She huffs and folds her arms across her chest.

"Did you summon us here so you can chitchat on your mobile or for some other reason?" She asks.

Again, I let her snide remark go for the sake of peace. Besides, I don't want my flight crew to overhear a personal conversation with my siblings. I shake my head at Signy and mouth, not now.

She sits back with a scowl and takes her mobile from her white leather Chanel backpack. Viggo and I exchange glances. He shrugs and pulls out his mobile. Fingers fly across the screen as he grins at whatever he reads. For the rest of the twenty-minute ride, our little sister ignores us.

Unlike Viggo, Signy doesn't work at Larson Enterprises. She lives the pampered life of the daughter of a former Alpha and sister to the current one. It's our fault since she's the only girl and the baby of our family at twenty-four, four years younger than me. The rest of us coddle her.

When our father wanted to strengthen an alliance with a pack out west, he told her she would mate their Alpha. For obvious reasons, she lacked attraction to the much older male whose mate had died and left him without an heir. Readily, Viggo and I stood up for her. We insisted she have more time to find her fated mate, just as our father did with our mother. He agreed, if reluctantly.

Now, I expect Signy to offer the same support for me. I

glance over at her as she rises to disembark from the helicopter. She still wears the scowl from earlier. I sigh.

Ordinarily, she's fun-loving with a good sense of humor. Smart and independent. A joy to be around. However, she still lives with our parents in their waterfront mansion on Moon Island. Named for our mother Sigrid—a Viking name for victory. Signy means new victory.

Well, I hope to triumph over her apparent disapproval of my mating with Sage.

Viggo follows Signy with a parting wink to the flight attendant. She blushes and busies herself with reordering the cabin. He chuckles. I chuff him in the back of the head and growl. He smirks. Fucker.

Signy stands with her hands on her hips.

"Are we doing this or what?" She calls out over the sound of the rotors as they power off.

"Good luck, bro," Viggo murmurs under his breath.

Yeah, tell me about it…

I glance around the area cleared for a helipad near our pack's camp in the Everglades. It's the place we come for pack runs and trainings. For generations, the virtually untouched area of the subtropical wilderness allows us the freedom to be in our wolf form without prying eyes. Over the years, the original pack grounds grew from temporary cloth shelters to simple wooden cabins and now to luxurious residences scattered around the Alpha's house and clubhouse. Glamping—or glamorous camping, as Signy —calls it.

A few families and enforcers choose to remain here, not wanting the hustle and bustle of Miami for their principal home. On days like this one when the humidity is low, the sun sits in a cloudless sky, and fresh air abounds, I don't blame them. My thoughts move to bringing my fated mate here for a few days to ourselves once everything settles, especially since we first met near to here.

"Greetings, Alpha!"

I turn to find the wolf shifter I put in charge of our property striding towards me. I shake his extended hand and clap him on the back.

"Good to see you, Ulf!" I respond.

"After your run, we'll have a good meal ready for you. My mate's excited to cook for our Alpha and his siblings. She's prepared some of her specialties just for you," he says with a broad smile.

"Thanks to you both. We appreciate a delicious home-cooked meal any day!"

I turn to my siblings and tell them to go to their cabins and leave their things before we shift, then meet outside of my cabin. They nod.

Once inside of my residence, I send a text message to my fated mate. She responds all is well. Relieved, I strip out of my t-shirt and jeans before I shift. My giant silvery white wolf pads to the door and slaps the button. The hand-carved wooden door depicting a wolf opens. I bound out to meet my siblings. My wolf yips in excitement to be free.

I run up to Signy's wolf—a black beauty with a white

patch on her back—and pug her flank where it's ticklish with my muzzle. Her stiff posture relaxes as I continue to poke her beast. After a while, she gives in and yips before hopping into the air, tongue lolling and eyes bright.

A wave of relief rolls over me at the sight of my little sister being her normal self with me. Then I stumble sideways. A glance over my shoulder reveals a red wolf with its lips pulled back in a toothy grin. Viggo!

I rush him and we tumble to the ground, rolling around like we did as pups—and still do occasionally. Signy's wolf bounces around us, getting in a nip to our flanks or rumps, dodging our swatting paws with ease. Then she yips and bounds towards the tree line.

Viggo and I give chase.

Hours after traipsing through the wetlands, hunting, and lying in the sun, we return to the cabins. We separate to shower and meet back at my cabin. Changed back into my t-shirt and jeans, I call Sage. She answers on the first ring.

"Hi! How's it going?"

I grin as her love flows through our tether, even at the distance of nearly thirty miles. My wolf thumps his tail in happiness.

"Good. I haven't spoken to Signy yet. But she loosened up once we shifted. Her wolf was easygoing. Hopefully she will be too."

We talk a bit longer until I hear my front door open and the voices of my siblings as they talk smack to each other. I ring off from my fated mate with promises to devour her tonight. I end the call to the sounds of her giggles, then bound down the stairs.

"Whatever, Viggo! You don't understand," Signy says as she punches him in the chest.

He doesn't flinch and shakes his head at her.

I glance between the two.

They clam up until I cock an eyebrow—Alpha command wafting off me.

They eye each other. Viggo arcs his hand through the air, signaling Signy to proceed. She growls at him and snaps her head in my direction.

"How could you, Jagger?! I mean, a witch? Really?! What a total mess! She's—" She yells as her ice blue eyes flash.

I cross my arms over my chest. I gave her leeway before. But no one will disrespect my fated mate. No. One.

"Signy, I suggest you consider your choice of words very carefully when you speak of my fated mate," I tell her, drawing on every ounce of my steely Alpha command.

My younger sister's eyes widen as her mouth flops open like a fish pulled from the water. She scans my face. Seeing no room for argument, she lowers her head and mutters to herself.

Naturally, my wolf senses pick up her words of 'arrogant,' 'selfish,' and 'not fair'. I wait for her to get herself together. She strides to the living room and throws herself onto a leather sofa. Eyes stare up at me.

"Jagger, Mom and Dad told me all about your *fated mate* and how you lost it over her years ago. They had to consider our pack over your... your... sexual desires," she says with a lip curled in disgust. "And now, you flaunt her in front of our pack and let her hurt Melissa?! How could you, Jagger?!"

Viggo steps forward, ready to defend me. I raise my hand to stop him. He slumps into a chair, disappointed eyes fixed on our younger sister.

I stride over to the sofa and sit beside her. Obviously, our parents filled her head with bullshit. Had she come to the meeting she would have heard my side of the situation, not one meant to cast my mating with Sage in a horrible light.

"Signy, do you truly believe me capable of whatever you were told I did?" I ask quietly as my eyes stare into hers.

She squirms under the intensity of my gaze and glances away. After a moment, she shifts her gaze back to mine. She studies my face.

I keep an open expression to allow her to see no deceit, only her brother, the one who cared for her all her life. Who wants nothing but the best for her.

"Well, that's what they told me," she responds at last.

I shake my head.

"Do you trust me, Signy?"

She hesitates, then nods.

"Well, then, let me tell you what really happened…"

Like the pack members in the meeting, Signy voices outrage at the lies our parents told her. She apologizes for not speaking to me before—believing their lies—and vows to support Sage and me. My little sister throws her arms around my shoulders when I forgive her.

I hold her close and thank her for standing by my side.

Viggo comes over and grabs us for a group hug. Signy's eyes shine through her tears as she expresses how grateful she is to have us as her big brothers.

A knock on the front door separates us. Ulf enters to let us know lunch is ready. We thank him, and he leaves.

I turn to my siblings and grab them close again. Our foreheads touch as I thank them for their love and support.

We stand as one. I can only hope Sage's siblings will continue to do the same for her.

 age

"HONEY! It's been a shitstorm up here. I came back as Tabitha returned from Miami. A category five hurricane, I tell you! She was beyond pissed! Even Rupert cowered at her rage"—Anala blows a breath before she continues—"The coven met to decide what to do. Of course, they gave me and others connected to you the side-eye. I know they had a second meeting to really discuss things. For now, they only said Rupert decided to take a sojourn through Europe for an indeterminate amount of time. To lick his wounds, no doubt…"

I listen as Anala fills me in on the reaction of the Northeast Coven to the news of me calling off the pairing with Rupert and mating with Jagger instead. It's worse than I thought. If it angered the second most powerful coven, the Witch Council will definitely get involved. I hope they'll listen to me and consider the part of Jagger and I being *fated* mates, and not some randy teens wanting to sate their desires despite the impact on others.

That's exactly why I'm so glad I followed my intuition and came back to The Waters Tower. I didn't use my teleportation magick. With my head held high and back straight, I entered through the lobby. From the valet to the doorman and the coven members milling about, they watched my every move. I acknowledged them with my regular greetings, not allowing them to see they fazed me at all.

Only within my penthouse duplex did I let the walls crumble. My body shook as I thought back on the hostile faces and recalled their snide remarks about me being a mangy wolf lover and forsaking my lineage and coven. It hurt me to my core. My own coven could turn on me so easily after knowing me all my life. And especially as their leader.

I didn't let on my dismay to Jagger whenever he sent a text message or called. It's best he focuses on his pack and reconnecting with his sister Signy, whom I haven't met yet since she's not thrilled about the pairing any more than my coven.

And I haven't heard from nor seen my parents and Willow. Who knows what they're up to? Their silence unnerves me. But my disappointment with Willow pains me even more.

I thought my own sister would stand beside me, show strength and support in the face of the covens and the Witch Council. But no. She's ghosted me. I never would have thought she'd ditch me.

My eyes close to block the pain. I take a deep cleansing breath to clear my head and tune back in to my bestie. At least Anala stays in my corner. She's my eyes and ears for the happenings up north, even if they hold secret meetings without her present. She's well respected in her coven. Hell, even feared by many. Anyone who can successfully kill vampires proves a force to be reckoned with.

"—shifters from the New York Wolves Pack slinking around me. When I caught them in a trap, they confessed Jagger asked their Alpha to watch my back. Give your mate my thanks. Even though I don't need their help, I appreciate his concern."

My heart swells with love for my mate, knowing he reached out to another powerful Alpha to look after my cousin. Jagger is so good to me. Suddenly, I get a burst of love through our tether from him. I was careful to suppress my sadness and let my happiness come through our bond. Thankfully, he only picked up on the positive and not the negative. I send my love to him and sit back with a smile on my face.

"Thanks so much, Anala. You don't know what it means to me you're sticking by Jagger and me. I don't want to cause any trouble between you and your coven. So, only do what you deem necessary. Don't push it on my account," I tell her.

She huffs. I can picture her eyes rolling as her full lips purse.

"Sage, never mind all that nonsense. What's right is right and what's wrong is wrong. Period. A fated mate bond is nothing to ignore or try to deny. I hope one day to meet my fated mate. And I tell you now, I won't let him go for anything. Nothing at all!"

"I'll remind you should you ever forget, Anala Azar," I say with a grin.

Voices outside my office at Sage's Gems & Jewels catch my attention. I tell Anala to hold on as I go see what's happening. Lillie stands toe to toe with Njal. The giant of a wolf shifter—his Viking name literally means giant and suits him perfectly—stares down at my younger sister impassively. She glares at him, then sees me at the open door.

"Sage! Tell this behemoth to let me into your office right this minute!" Lillie exclaims as she stomps her Manolo Blahnik covered foot and points her finger up at Njal.

I stifle a giggle at her tiny frame compared to his, well, giant one. Then beckon for her to come in. I wink at Njal over her head. His face contorts into what may be his version of a smile but resembles a grimace. I close the door and shake my head as I raise my mobile to my ear.

"Hey, Anala, Lillie just came in. I'll call you later. Thanks again," I say.

"Anytime, honey. Tell Lil I said hi!" Anala responds before she ends the call.

I relay the message as I follow Lillie to the sofa. She nods. A worried expression mars her pretty face.

"Talk to me, Lillie, and don't hold back. I want to hear all you have to say," I tell her as I clasp her hand and squeeze. I sit back and wait.

Between her slender fingers, she twists the hem of her Roland Mouret dress. Distress clearly outlined on her face as she opens, then closes her mouth. She shakes her head, and her mane of ebony hair falls across her profile like a silky curtain. She sighs, then shifts on the sofa to face me.

"Sage, I love you so much and hate what Mother did to you and Jagger. She was wrong to go about it the way she did."

My heart sinks. Lillie—my little sister—would have preferred a different method to block me from my fated mate? Oh dear, this is not good at all. I bite my tongue to prevent myself from speaking.

She continues, unaware of the pain she just inflicted on my heart.

"I mean, Mother should have given you a chance to defend yourselves, at least listen to you before going to such extremes. Erasing your memories? For ten years? Wow! Just wow."

Lillie reaches for my hand, and I let her take it. She doesn't notice how limp it dangles in hers. She squeezes.

"Jagger seems like a really great… uh… wolf shifter. I'm sure he cares for you. But do you think it's worth it? To have our coven, the Northeast Coven, and undoubtedly his pack in an uproar for just the two of you? It's kind of self-ish. You know what I mean, Sage?"

I yank my hand from hers and sit up.

"No, Lillie, I do not know what you mean! What I know is you've changed your mind and want to clear your guilt by making me think I'm the one who's wrong. I. Am. Not. What I am is surprised at you and at Willow. How many times did I have your backs when Mother tried to run your lives? How many times did I bite the bullet and take the brunt of her demands to keep my *little sisters* free from her? Need I remind you? And Willow? Wherever the hell she may be! Anala—our *cousin*—has my back and my *sisters* do not."

To hell with this bullshit!

I snatch my mobile from the coffee table as I jump to my feet, then storm to my desk. Ignoring Lillie's sobs, I put my laptop in my handbag and head for the double doors. I open and close them without a backwards glance at my sister seated on the sofa still.

Njal takes one look at my face and having heard our conversation with his enhanced wolf hearing nods and gestures for the other enforcers. He leads the way to the elevator. As we walk through my boutique, I send a text message to the manager letting her know I've gone home and will be unavailable until tomorrow.

I keep my head high and back straight as I walk surrounded by my wolf shifter security detail past humans, witches, and any other paranormal beings who bustle about The Waters Tower Mall. But the moment the door closes on the Suburban, I shrink into the soft leather with my face in my hands and cry.

JAGGER

PAIN PIERCES my heart so deeply I choke and press my palm to my chest.

Sage!

I jump from my chair at the table where my siblings, other pack members, and I sit after eating lunch. My hands fumble in my jeans pocket for my mobile. I press her number conveniently saved in favorites since my hands shake with the powerful urge to shift and free my wolf, who howls.

A few rings come across the line before she answers just as I was about to call Njal. I sigh in relief, then snarl when I hear her tear-choked voice warble.

"J—J—Jagger…" she cries pitifully before a sob breaks over the line.

I turn to the table. Viggo has his mobile to his ear as he stands beside Signy. Her worried eyes scan my face. Viggo motions for me to follow.

"The flight crew heads to the helicopter now," he says, eyes flashing silver, then he turns to Ulf. "Thanks for lunch."

Signy rubs my arm as her long legs trot to keep pace with my long strides.

"Whatever it is, Jagger, we have your back. Don't worry, big brother," she says vehemently.

I nod as I turn my attention back to my fated mate.

"Where are you? Are you hurt? What happened?" I bark.

She takes a breath and tells me she's in the SUV with Njal and is safe. As she recounts her conversation with Lillie, my blood boils and my wolf claws at my skin to break free. I tamp him down as we board the helicopter. No one needs my wild wolf pacing within the confines of the helicopter, no matter how spacious it is.

No sooner does the flight attendant close the door than the pilot lifts off. We zip back to Miami in less than twenty minutes. All the while, I soothe my fated mate. The helicopter hovers over our side lawn just as her Suburban pulls into our driveway. With a nod to my siblings, I jump out and roll as I hit the grass, then leap to my feet, running for the side door.

"Sage!" I bellow as the door slams into the plaster. Pieces fall to the tile as I rush to find her. I sigh in relief when she hurtles towards me and flings herself into my outstretched arms. "Oh, baby, baby. It's okay. I'm here now."

I croon to her as she trembles. Her sisters really did her wrong. And I thought Signy was a lost cause.

Over Sage's head, I notice Njal. He watches with a steely glint in his gray eyes. His wolf also flexes beneath the surface of his skin.

It pleases me he cares so much for my fated mate and his Luna. I nod and send him my thanks through the bond I have as Alpha with my pack. His massive chest rises on an inhalation as he wrestles control of his wolf. He returns my nod and spins on his heel to leave the mansion.

"Come on, baby, let me take you upstairs. I'll draw us a nice bath so we can soak. Okay, baby?" I murmur against the top of Sage's head. She nods, and I scoop her up. I call out for the smart home system to run the bath water with essential oils.

By the time I carry her into my bathroom, the tub is full of warm water ready for us. I set Sage on the navy blue terrycloth bench in the center of the bathroom. I cup her face and kiss her lips softly before I put cool water on a washcloth and dab her tear-stained face. She closes her eyes and leans into my gentle touch.

We undress each other as I rumble deep in my chest to soothe my fated mate. Her eyes aren't so much sad anymore as they are resigned. I hate she feels that way, but I don't pressure her to talk now. It's time for our bodies to speak the only words necessary. Those declarations of the special love only a fated pair can know.

And to hell with anyone who doesn't understand.

Once we're naked, I carry her to the bath and step in. Keeping her close to my chest, I lean my back against the side of the copper bathtub, then arrange her in front of me with her back to my front. My long, muscular legs stretch out along the sides of her slim ones. I keep my arms wrapped around her, just beneath her full breasts.

My lips trail open-mouthed kisses along the side of her neck.

Sage leans into me and rests her arms on top of mine. She tilts her head to give me better access to the column of her throat. She moans as I press my lips to my claiming bite. The wound healed nicely, allowing the mark to show clearly.

As I cup her breasts now heavy in my hands, she mewls and drags her fingernails over my scalp. I shudder from the erotic pain. My already turgid cock thumps against her spine. I pinch and tug at her nipples, gauging her desire.

She moves swiftly to straddle my thighs. Water sloshes to the marble floor. She reaches between us and fists my cock. Her thumb rubs over the mushroom head as she rises to her knees to align the tip with her pussy.

We groan in unison as it breaches her folds and she sinks back onto my thighs. Her hips circle to help with the tight fit as her inner walls clamp and drag my cock deep inside. I grab her hips and pull her down as I thrust up. She throws her head back and cries out my name. My mouth closes around a pebbled brown nipple presented to me as her breasts rise. Her hips undulate as I suckle.

Her fingernails dig into my shoulders as she finds her rhythm. Up and down, she bounces on my cock as she rides out her frustration. I hold her hips to keep her balanced and meet each of her violent slams with a brutal thrust of my own. My hooded eyes eat up the sight of my gorgeous fated mate. I'm more than happy to endure her vexation.

With a guttural moan, she climaxes and falls forward, face buried in my neck. Warm pants lick across my sweaty skin. Her tight, little pussy spasms along my cock, choking my release from my heavy balls.

I yank her down and grind up until I bottom out. A feral roar rips from my throat as I unleash a torrent of my seed in her womb. White light dazzles behind my eyelids, squeezed shut as the orgasm rages on. The aftereffects ripple through me, refusing to end. I take them with low groans slipping from my slack mouth.

After we return to Earth, I bathe my fated mate, then myself. I dry us off before wrapping us in heated terrycloth robes and carrying her to our bed. I pull the cashmere blanket from the foot to cover us. She cuddles against me with her cheek and palm on my chest. I rub her back and rumble to her.

"The coven and the Witch Council want me to step down and Willow to take over and pair with Rupert."

Well, I'll be damned.

age

"IT'S ALL RIGHT, Jagger. I just need to walk and clear my head. And if you feel anything over our bond, don't worry and let me be. Lots of emotions will well up, I'm sure. But I'll be fine and won't leave Moon Island. Promise."

My super-protective fated mate narrows his ice blue eyes as he scans my face. He wants to keep me in our bayfront mansion until the meeting later today. I tell him not to worry. The witches can't harm me or get to me here.

I placed protective wards around Moon Island, the Everglades camp, and Larson Enterprises. Now that I'm a part of the pack—their Luna—it's my responsibility to keep them safe with my magick. Despite Jagger's knowledge of my precautions, concern mars his handsome face.

I lift my hand and cup his cheek as I send calm through our tether.

He closes his eyes and leans into my palm with a sigh. Emotions play across his face as he considers my words. Eyebrows dip, nostrils flare, lips move in silent internal debate. Finally, resignation. His eyes open to pin me with an intense stare.

"Fine. But Njal will follow you"—he raises his hand at my protest—"he'll keep his distance. Or you can stay here. Any one of the many rooms can provide the space you need."

Quickly, I shake my head and agree to Njal's shadow. Then press a kiss to Jagger's full lips. His tongue darts out to deepen the connection, but I pull back with a wry smile. My fated mate won't lock lips to prevent me from leaving. No, ma'am!

He growls low in his chest as I dart away. I wiggle my fingers over my shoulder as I hurry towards the side door. No more than a few steps outside and I sense Njal behind me. I glance back. Yup, the Giant follows. I offer him a smile, and he inclines his head.

As I follow the stone-paved path beneath palm trees, I close my eyes and let the floral fragrances of the gardenia and jasmine bushes fill my nose. The scents mingle with the saltwater air wafting in from the Atlantic Ocean. The splash from the wake of jet skis as they fly by and the horn of a cruise ship drift in from Biscayne Bay a few yards away.

Being on Moon Island feels like a whole other world

separate from the bustle of Miami around it. A serene oasis filled with lush foliage provides the perfect respite. And that's what I need to prepare myself for the meeting.

I still can't believe the phone call I received from my mother as I rode from The Waters Tower to Moon Island. She told me as the prior High Witch it was her duty to inform me of the coven and Witch Council's recommendation and of my opportunity to speak before them. Recommendation? Bullshit!

The brief interlude broken, my eyes snap open as I fist my hands and storm forward.

How dare they *recommend* ousting me and replacing me with my own sister? How could she accept? Whose bright idea was it to begin with? Prudence? Tabitha? Rupert? Hell, Willow???

I tromp along the path, barely aware of my surroundings. Wild thoughts run through my mind on a loop.

Should I refuse and fight back? What if I ignore their *recommendation* and carry on as usual? Should I seek supporters within the witches and stage a revolt? Would the wolf shifters back me?

I throw my head back and scream until I have to stop for a breath.

Aargh!

Birds startle and take flight from the palm trees. Lizards dive from the path into the underbrush. A few members in wolf form howl.

My skin feels tight. Fingers twitch. I glance around and

find I'm a few yards from the bay. The sparking azure blue water calls to me. With a wave of my hand, the tank top and yoga pants morph into a teal blue bikini as I race forward.

The minute my feet touch the water, a sense of relaxation washes through me. I scramble over the slippery rocks to reach where it's deeper. Raising my arms overhead, hands together, I dive in. The sound of Njal's gruff voice calling my name fades as the water covers my ears.

My element cleanses me with each vigorous stroke as I swim parallel to Moon Island. The source of my magick binds with me. It covers my skin and fills every cell. My heartbeat thrums boldly in my chest. I swim faster as I circle the island. Time and distance become meaningless as I lose myself in the revitalizing water.

When I rise from Biscayne Bay, my mind is free from turmoil and my body vibrates with renewed power. Peace fills me. I am ready.

Njal stands at the edge of the grass. He watches me as I stride towards him. Not one to talk, he nods when he's satisfied I'm okay. I return his nod and continue to the path.

I let the water seep into my skin as I head back to the mansion. When I step onto the stone pavers, an older wolf shifter greets me with a respectful nod. When he lifts his face, I recognize him as Bo from the pack meeting. I smile and extend my hand.

"Hello, Bo. I'm glad to see you. I want to thank you for your kind words at the pack meeting. Do you have a moment to speak with me? I'd like to ask you about how you knew my grandmother."

"Yes, Luna. In fact, I came to speak to you. I understand you have a meeting with the coven and the Witch Council?" He takes my hand and pauses for confirmation.

I'm shocked he knows. Only witches were told about it. I doubt any of them would have leaked negative information about the coven, especially to a wolf shifter. I don't ask who told him and confirm the meeting.

He nods and gestures for us to walk.

"If you do not mind, Luna, I would like to attend the meeting as your guest. And obviously as your and the Alpha's supporter," Bo says.

Again, he catches me by surprise. But Jagger and I could use all the support we can get and show a united front to the witches.

"Absolutely, Bo. Jagger and I would appreciate you standing with us. You're a respected elder of the Miami Wolves Pack. Your opinion holds value. The meeting is at one. We can pick you up on our way to The Waters Tower."

Bo shakes his head.

"Unnecessary, Luna. I will meet you at your residence. Until then," he says, then bows his head and walks the other way.

I watch him go. He nods at Njal, then continues down the path.

Well, that was a welcome surprise, I muse to myself. We can add Bo to our list, along with Anala, who told me she'll be there ready to rumble. The corners of my mouth begin to lift, then spread into a broad smile.

The better it gets, the better it gets.

My step is light as I continue on to the mansion. A few feet from the side door and it opens wide. Jagger stalks out, a scowl on his face.

"Sage! Where are your clothes?! You walked around the island in a skimpy ass bikini?!"

I throw my head back and laugh.

Correction, my super-*possessive* fated mate…

"You okay, baby?"

Jagger squeezes my hand resting on his thick thigh as we ride in his Black Badge Rolls-Royce Cullinan bound for The Waters Tower. His ice blue eyes filled with concern study my face.

I cup his cheek and smile.

"Yes, my love. I will fight for my positions and not allow them to take what is rightfully mine. I've worked too hard and been too good of a leader for them to think they can toss me aside over their narrow-minded beliefs."

My fated mate grins and presses his forehead to mine.

"And I'm right by your side, mate of mine," he murmurs.

"We're here, Alpha."

Karl's voice draws Jagger and me from our bubble. He nods and presses his lips to mine. Then sits back and straightens the knot of his silk tie.

The doors open, and we step out of the SUV. I close my eyes and take a deep breath. Instantly, the sounds of waves breaking on the shore fill my head. My element seeks to calm me and maintain my strength.

Jagger takes my hand and cocks an eyebrow. I nod reassuringly, and his shoulders relax, if only slightly. He turns and—with an air of determination—leads me to the front doors of The Tower.

Not only Bo joined us for support. Viggo and Signy—who I met briefly as we climbed into the SUV—came to support their brother. Tag and Rust stand with their best friend. While Karl, Njal and some other enforcers provide security.

The doorman's mouth gapes like a fish floundering for air. We stride by him as he holds the door open. I feel his eyes drilling into the back of my skull as I go through the lobby, headed for the elevators. I draw up to my full height, not allowing the weight of his glare to drag me down.

At the elevators, our group splits to enter two cars. We reach the floor for the coven's grand hall simultaneously. Witches who linger in the lobby turn to stare. They point and whisper, eyes wide at the arrival of several wolf shifters.

Two of the members who function as security step in front of me. Eyes full of menace.

Jagger steps between us as Viggo, Tag, Rust, and Karl flank him. Njal and the enforcers stand beside Signy and me.

"Move away from my mate," Jagger growls. His wolf roams beneath the surface.

"You have no right to be here," Morris, one witch, says. "Leave now."

"Morris, unless you wish me to cast you from your rank, back away. Now," I say as I step between Jagger and Tag.

Morris sneers and responds, "You have no autho—"

I silence him with a flick of my wrist. His hands fly to his closed mouth. Eyes wide, he pokes the sealed seam of his lips in an attempt to part them. I narrow my eyes at him and scan the faces of those gathered.

"I have every bit of *authority* as I am the leader of this coven and the High Witch. Do not disrespect me, my fated mate, or my pack," I say fervently.

Silence ensues.

I take Jagger's hand and step forward. He tightens his grip and walks beside me. The rest of our pack follows. Inside the grand hall, more stares and murmurs greet us. I ignore them as I continue to the dais.

A row of chairs stands before it, separate from those for the coven. Members of the Witch Council turn in the chairs to watch our approach. My mother, father, Lillie, Tabitha, and members of the Northeast Coven sit amongst them. Willow sits in her seat beside my chair on the dais.

For a moment, my heart constricts. Jagger squeezes my hand and sends love through our bond. I square my shoulders. The sounds of waves increase. You've got this, Sage! I cheer myself.

"Sage! Jagger!"

I pause and turn towards my bestie's voice.

Anala blazes a trail through the crowd behind us. Her chocolate brown eyes shine with her internal fire. My pack makes room for her to reach me. She pulls me into a hug, then smiles up at Jagger.

"I saved seats for everyone right behind them," she says with a glare at the others. Some of the council members have the grace to lower their eyes. "You take your *rightful seat*, Sage. I put a chair behind yours for Jagger, your *fated mate*. The rest of you come with me."

My heart swells with love for Anala. She winks at me and leads my pack to their seats.

"Come on, baby," Jagger murmurs low so only I can hear.

I nod and press on.

Those seated in the additional row know better than to question me and say nothing as Jagger and I pass them. We settle in our seats. I nod at Willow. She hesitates, then returns my polite gesture. I look out at those seated in the grand hall.

Quickly, the last of them take their seats. I turn to the secretary, and she nods.

"Good afternoon. It is 1:00, and I call the meeting of the Coven of the South to order."

After the secretary calls each member's name and marks those present, I'm not surprised to find all members in attendance. Each visitor stands and gives their name. My pack follows once the witches speak. The secretary adds them to the list on her laptop. When she finishes, she announces the number present.

Here we go…

"As you may know, Prudence Waters, the prior High Witch informed me of the coven and of the Witch Council's recommendation. They wish for me to step down as leader of the Coven of the South, High Witch, and head of the Witch Council. They wish for Willow Waters of the Coven of the South to replace me and to pair with Rupert Ravenheart of the Northeast Coven."

Who's notably absent, I muse to myself.

Silence encompasses the vast space.

"First, I ask the speaker for them to stand and explain their reasoning. Then I will respond," I say, and shift my gaze to those seated in the additional row.

Their heads turn to my mother, of course.

Prudence rises from her chair. Her emerald green eyes focused on mine. It's incredible how much we resemble each other. Thankfully, I did not inherit her stony heart. She nods at me, then pivots to face those gathered.

"Thank you to all who came out for this unexpected situation," she says and pauses as she turns her gaze to individuals. "Sage Waters has turned her back on her coven, her fiancé, and all witches for the most selfish reason. Her lust-filled desire drove her to mate with a *wolf shifter*."

Amidst the cries of the coven, Jagger's anger bears down on our bond as he struggles to maintain control of himself and of his wolf. Ferocity pours from his body. I glance at our pack as they stir, feeling his ire through their connection. Jagger takes a ragged breath as he wins the battle.

I sigh in relief. We need to remain cool and calm. I send my plea through our tether. He nods.

"We do not agree with Sage's decision, as it is not conducive for the wellbeing of the Coven of the South or for the role of the High Witch and head of the Witch Council. In addition, her selfish decision negatively impacts the relationship between the Coven of the South and the Northeast Coven. We stand by our recommendation and put it forth to the Coven of the South to vote, then to the Witch Council."

She turns to me with a gleam in her eyes and continues.

"We have witnesses who wish to be heard."

I meet her gaze with a cool one of my own.

"They may speak now."

She nods her head at a witch who stands beside the side door. She opens it, and Jagger growls low.

I watch, shocked, as his parents step into the grand hall. Signy gasps in the silence. But I keep my eyes on Marcus and Sigrid.

They shift glares between Jagger and me. Then a snarl rips from Marcus' curled lip when he sees Viggo and Signy standing.

"You dare to defy your father?" He bellows at his daughter.

Signy lifts her chin and responds, "I stand by my brother and my Alpha, Jagger, and his *fated* mate, Sage."

"As do I," Viggo growls.

The rest of the pack jump to their feet and voice their support.

Reluctantly, I raise my hand and call for order. They settle down immediately. I turn to Marcus and Sigrid.

"You may speak."

He steps closer. But Jagger rises and growls, "That's as far as you will go." They lock eyes. Jagger's power as current Alpha thwarts his father. He curls his lip. But stays where he stands. He turns to the crowd.

"I am Marcus Larson, the immediate past Alpha of the Miami Wolves Pack. We do not condone the mating of—"

"You do not speak for the pack. We held the meeting you did not attend, and they recognize Sage as their Luna. Do not challenge me, or you will fail," Jagger declares, standing tall beside me.

The males glower at one another. Once again, Marcus bows before Jagger's strength. He steps back.

Prudence jumps to her feet.

"How dare you run our coven's meeting, *wolf shifter*?" She shouts, emerald eyes flashing. She spins on her heels and faces the grand hall. "This is exactly what we fear. The *wolf shifter* will control Sage and thus the coven, council, and all witches! We must end this threat now!"

The space erupts with shouts.

I stand and silence them all.

"No one shall speak unless recognized as per the rules of decorum of this coven," I say. When they nod in compliance, I release the spell and turn to my mother.

"Are you finished with your explanation for your recommendation, Prudence?"

"Yes, I am!"

I ignore her snippy tone.

"We have heard you. Now, you may sit," I tell her and wait to take my seat until she sits on hers. With a huff, she lowers herself. I return to my chair.

"My response is such witches abide by the rules set forth by our ancestors, rules adapted as time requires. Such as changing the rule only witches of the same gender may mate to allow any gender to be as one. Regarding witches mating with wolf shifters or any non-witch being, nowhere in the histories of this coven or in any of the ancient witch texts does such rule exist."

I turn my gaze to those in the additional row.

"Your recommendation is not valid, as I have broken no rule by mating with Jagger Larson."

They huddle and murmur amongst themselves.

"Excuse me, Luna and High Witch, may I speak as a witness?"

I glance over at Bo. This elder continues to surprise me.

"Yes, Bo, respected elder of the Miami Wolves Pack, we may hear you," I respond.

He steps before the dais and faces the grand hall.

"Yes, I am a respected elder of the Miami Wolves Pack. And I am also a descendant of a female witch of the Coven of the South and a former beta of the pack—"

Witches and wolf shifters speak at once.

I'm so shocked, I forget to correct the outburst. Jagger

nudges me, and I snap to.

"Silence! Now!"

The noise dies down, and I gesture for Bo to continue.

"Thank you, Luna and High Witch. I know this may surprise most of you. However, a few of you know more than you care to admit, obviously. Besides myself, there are more like me everywhere than you realize. Is that not so, Eliphas, Holly, Blaise?"

Bo pauses to point out several witches, even one on the Witch Council. Their mouths open but they think better of it and remain silent. He shakes his head, disappointed at their reluctance to admit their lineage.

"The stigma associated with the love between a wolf shifter and a witch forces those pairs and their offspring to hide, even in plain sight. Those spurned also carry a grudge and try to prevent others the love they themselves could not have. Isn't that correct, Cyrus?"

The most vocal witch now sits hunched in his chair, silent, while his eyes shoot daggers at Bo.

"Luna and High Witch, I knew your grandmother, a powerful woman who thought for herself"—he throws a glance at my mother and shakes his head sadly—"she would never have condoned the actions of those opposed to your mating with our Alpha. In fact, she told me of the foretold prophecy of a wolf shifter and a witch fated mates whose pairing will change the course of both pack and coven and whose offspring will rule both."

Now, even I gasp aloud along with others. Jagger takes my hand. We look at each other, unable to speak.

Bo clears his throat, and the space falls silent. Everyone leans forward to listen. Again, he turns to my mother.

"I am surprised you did not know since they passed the knowledge down in secret from one High Witch to the next," he says and waits for her response.

She lowers her eyes and whispers, "I know."

I jump to my feet and rush across the dais. Caught off guard, Jagger catches up to me and takes my arm.

"Why? Why would you erase our memories and cloak my scent if you knew, mother?! How could you?!" I shout.

She winces.

"I didn't want the prophecy to come to pass. It's just not right!"

My father rises and towers over my mother.

"Prudence Waters, you had no *right*! You are wrong! You abused your power and nearly ruined our daughter. I will no longer stand for you to hurt her for *your selfish* reasons!" He says as his voice rises in anger.

"Nor will I!" Lillie says as she throws a withering look at our mother and rushes to my side. She takes my hand and presses it to her forehead. "I am so sorry, Sage, Jagger, please, *please* forgive me!"

"We forgive you, Lillie," Jagger and I say in unison.

"Me, too."

The small voice comes from behind us. We turn to find Willow with tears streaming down her cheeks as she hurries towards us. She throws her arms around my neck and sobs as she begs for my forgiveness.

I hug her tightly and cry along with her. Lillie throws

her arms around both of us.

"Sister's group hug!" She says through her tears.

"Well, this is all fine and dandy for you all. However, my coven expects recompense."

I blink to clear the tears from my eyes before I face the leader of the Northeast Coven.

"Tabitha, the plan you and my mother designed for my life failed. There is no coming between fated mates. Any witch will be happy to have Rupert as a mate. But do not expect me to force anyone to pair with him as recompense. I expect our covens to continue amicably, as we have for centuries. Do you have an issue with that expectation?"

She flicks her gaze at Willow.

My sister moves behind me and Jagger's bulky frame. I reach back and touch her hip to let her know I have her back. I wait for Tabitha to speak.

She sucks in a breath and exhales slowly.

"No, Sage, I do not have an issue. Our covens will continue in harmony with yours. You have my word," Tabitha says as she inclines her head.

I return the gesture of respect.

"Wonderful," I respond, then turn to the grand hall. "Does anyone else wish to step forward as a witness or to object?"

Not a beat passes before someone claps. Others pick up the applause until it thunders around the grand hall.

"Well done, *mate*," Jagger murmurs in my ear.

I shiver and bite the corner of my lip.

Further correction, my super-*sexy-as-sin* fated mate.

 age

"I NEVER WANTED any part of your roles or to pair with Rupert. Eewww!"

Willow scrunches her dainty nose as her eyebrows dip.

"Oh, yuck! No sloppy seconds for this female!" Lillie adds with a grimace on her lovely face.

I laugh at the Twins not just because of the faces they make. But because we're back together again, as sisters should be always. Stand by one another as one. Sure, we'll have disagreements—hopefully none as big as the last fiasco. However, we'll not lose sight of what we are to one another.

It's been a week since the coven meeting. Jagger and I stayed at my penthouse duplex the first few days to make sure the coven remained stable and no one incited any animosity. Several members came to speak with me in private to express their concerns, whether for or against Jagger and me.

However, all were respectful and left with a better understanding of us as fated mates and less negativity towards wolf shifters. I'd rather they speak with me than plot behind my back. Fortunately, no one brought up my removal from my positions.

Bo's disclosure did a lot to change many minds—witch and wolf shifter. He stayed in one of the guest apartments and met with coven members, particularly the elders who knew my grandmother. His revelation of the prophecy surprised them—but none more than Jagger and me.

Jagger had him repeat every detail of the prophecy. The idea of a wolf shifter and a witch fated mates whose pairing will change the course of both pack and coven and whose offspring will rule both intrigued him.

I could sense from our tether his excitement for me to become pregnant. I'm surprised with all the lovemaking we've done—with and without his knot locking our pelvises—I'm not with child. It makes me a bit nervous. But I know the Fates have plans for us that supersede ours. My mother and Tabitha can vouch for that!

Prudence...

I haven't seen my mother since she left the grand hall. Her face covered in shame as those around her whispered about her actions. She attempted to keep a straight face. But her body language spoke volumes. Aa tightness around her eyes, shoulders slumped slightly, back not ramrod straight. Subtle differences to her normal formidable carriage I could detect.

Conversely, my father pulled Jagger and me aside right then and apologized profusely. He even expressed regret for allowing my mother to run my life for years. He allowed it because she reminded him she was in control constantly. So, he focused on Waters Corporation. He pledged himself to me and vowed to stand up to my mother should she seek to overthrow my positions. We thanked him, and he left to find my mother.

Sigrid approached us after my father stepped away. The former Luna and Jaggers' mother asked to make amends with us since the prophecy changed her mind. Her hazel eyes were full of remorse as she stared at her son's hard expression.

I let Jagger take the lead on this one. It's up to him should he forgive his parents. But Sigrid—like my father—seems to have followed what her mate told her. So, I'm inclined to accept her apology. Jagger is still undecided.

His father… Well, not so much.

Marcus refused to join us when Sigrid beckoned to him. He glared at me, then at Jagger, when he issued a warning growl. With a snarl, his father spun on his heels and left the grand hall. Sigrid offered excuses for him and hurried after her mate. We haven't heard from them. Viggo told us they flew to their residence in Key West. Jagger shrugged, disinterested in his parents or their whereabouts.

"And who the hell would want Rupert, anyway? He's always creeped me out. I'm telling you, something sinister always lingers in those obsidian eyes of his."

Anala's comment pulls me from my musings.

My cousin and bestie never wavered from my side—ride or die. And I love her for it. After the meeting, she popped back up to New York. She even used her teleportation to get there fast and not the commercial planes she prefers. She only returned yesterday and told me the Northeast Coven was not pleased with no replacement by one of my sisters for Rupert. But the legacy intrigued them.

Enough so that some of their members came forward to admit their descendancy from witches and shifters, even some of the big cat shifters. As it turns out, word spread amongst all the covens and more admitted their connections. I believe Bo reached out to them and urged them to step forward.

When he joined Jagger and me for dinner the other night, Bo explained more of his background. He's not fully immortal but can live much longer than wolf shifters. Silver does not kill him because of the witch's blood in his body. He said more like him will feel comfortable coming forward now with the most powerful Alpha wolf shifter and High Witch as a fated pair. Bo asserted we will have their support. We told him they will have ours. He said he's just pleased the prophecy has come to fruition.

I smile in the mirror as I agree with him wholeheartedly.

My white maxi dress floats around me as I twirl on bare

feet to get a glimpse of all angles. The gossamer light fabric shows just a hint of my body's curves. The strapless neckline shows off my fated mate's claiming bite. White jasmine flowers twine through my loose curls. Their symbolism of love, beauty, and sensuality sum up this moment perfectly.

The mate bonding ceremony between my fated mate and me.

Jagger and I will proclaim our love and commitment to one another in front of our families, closest friends, and members of our pack and coven. We decided to have a more intimate affair for this special occasion. Our formal wedding will happen in a few months, with invitations sent to the six wolf shifter packs, covens across the globe, and to the Witch Council. Already RSVPs have returned, with everyone responding yes. We'll hold it at a Larson Enterprises property in Miami.

But our mate bonding ceremony? Only one place can serve for us—the Everglades.

We're bringing it back to where it all began ten years ago. When a young witch and a young wolf shifter first experienced the love and passion of their fated mate. Where Jagger made me his. Now we complete our bond as one.

"Sage? Are you ready yet?"

Signy enters the sitting area of the primary bedroom suite in Jagger's cabin. My future sister-in-bond smiles at me as her ice blue eyes take in my dress.

"You look amazing, sis! I—I can't believe it," she says as tears shine in her eyes. "Jagger waited so long to find you, then lost you, and now you're together. Oh, Fates! I hope I can find my fated mate soon."

Willow, Lillie, and Anala throw their arms around her as they too express the desire for their fated mates. I beam as I watch my closest family take to one another so easily. Then say a prayer to the Fates my girls will find the unequivocal love I share with Jagger.

Another knock at the door, and I call for them to enter.

Prudence Waters. My mother.

Aargh!

She must see the dismay in my face because she rushes forward with her hands up, palms facing out. She's stopped by my girls as they place themselves between her and me.

"Sage, please, I—I don't mean any harm. I want to apologize and wish you well. Jagger—"

"I said she can come to you, and I will be right behind her—"

"NOOO!"

"Jagger! You can't see Sage before the ceremony!"

"Don't come in, Jagger!"

"Go back, brother!"

He chuckles and the double doors open despite Signy and Anala putting their weight against them. But instead of Jagger, Njal enters the room. The Giant steps between my mother and me. He folds his bulging arms across his massive chest and stares down at her. He stands at least a foot taller than her five foot, seven inches.

She blinks, then gazes around him with pleading eyes on me.

"Have your say, Mother."

She nods and licks her full lips.

"Sage, I was wrong and should never have done what I did to you or to Jagger. My fear and bias towards wolf shifters blinded me. I understand now how very wrong I was. I can only hope with time you will forgive me and allow me to be the mother I should have been to you all along."

Tears slip from her eyes. And in them I find no guile, nor do I sense ill will from her. I use my magick to double check. Nothing bad. I nod.

"I accept your apology, Mother—"

"So do I," Jagger says from behind the doors. "But if you don't mind, I want to complete the mate bonding ceremony. Now."

Everyone laughs at his demand. Even Njal's lips twitch. He guides my mother from the suite. She glances over her shoulder at me as he hustles her out. A watery smile lights her emerald green eyes. I smile back. With a wave, she's gone.

"Now, *mate*!" Jagger says with his Alpha command.

I jolt as it hits me.

"Yes, my love. We'll be right out."

"Ready, Sage?"

I glance up at the sound of my father's voice. He smiles at me as he enters the sitting room.

"How beautiful you look, sweetheart," he says as his eyes shine with unshed tears. "You're my first daughter to have her mate bonding ceremony. You make me so proud to be your father."

I take the tissue Willow hands to me and dab at my eyes. So much happiness flows through me at this moment.

"Come, Sage. Unless you want that mate of yours to storm in here and carry you to the ceremony bower," my father says with a raised eyebrow.

I giggle and loop my arm through his.

"As much as I love for my fated mate to carry me, I'd rather walk to meet him at our ceremony bower."

My girls go ahead of us and out the door of the cabin.

Although Jagger and I wanted to have our ceremony in the Everglades, we decided to keep our special place by the pond private. So, as my father guides me out the door, my eyes land on my fated mate a few yards away at the center of the camp.

Across the distance, his ice blue eyes pierce my very soul. So full of love and longing, I blush. The tether pulsates with his emotions. I return them tenfold. He smirks.

My father and I don't make it far down the aisle before Jagger stalks forward and lifts me in his arms with a possessive growl. He rumbles in his chest as I wrap my arms around his neck and bury my face against his skin.

The guests clap and stomp their feet. Wolf whistles fill the air. Suddenly, white jasmine petals fall all around us. Their fragrance mingles with that of the wetlands.

I glance up to find my mother smiling as her fingers wiggle

in the air, causing more flowers to shift in the breeze. I mouth thank you, and she bows her head. A symbol of peace I'm grateful for since I never wanted to battle with my mother.

"Time to complete our bond, *mate.*"

Jagger's husky baritone sends shivers down my spine. I shudder in his arms and tighten my grip around his neck.

"Yes, mate!" I respond enthusiastically.

He chuckles and strides towards the ceremony bower made from items found in the Everglades. Branches, twigs, driftwood, and colorful wildflowers mix for a beautiful bower. He lowers me to my feet, and we face one another, hands clasped together.

"Sage Waters, I claim you as my fated mate to protect, love, and cherish for all time. To bear my pups and to lead our pack with me as the Luna. I love you, Sage Larson Waters, my fated mate!"

I swallow back tears of joy, then clear my throat to respond.

"Jagger Larson, I claim you as my fated mate to protect, love, and cherish for all time. To bear your pups and to lead our pack with you, our Alpha. I love you, Jagger Waters Larson, my fated mate!"

The clearing explodes with shouts and howls of jubilation.

Jagger lifts me in the air and swings me around. I throw my head back and give my best howl. He joins me for a song of love. Then he carries me back up the aisle and straight to our cabin. More wolf whistles and howls punch through the air.

"Jagger! Where are you going?"

"Taking you into seclusion for a week, *mate*," he growls, with eyes flashing as his wolf rises to the surface.

"But our guests… lunch…"

"MINE! NOW!"

He pushes the door open with his foot and races up the stairs three at a time. I hold on as I giggle.

But when my fated mate strips me of my ceremony gown, I'm no longer laughing. Only lustful moans, mewls, and screams of his name fall from my mouth. His knot swells behind the wall of my core to lock us together. The first jettison of his seed shoots deep into my core. Instantly, a spark glimmers in my womb, and I gasp.

CHAPTER 20

 *agger*

"Hɪ, baby. What are you doing out here? You know you can't run off like that, *mate*."

Sage smiles at me as I scoop her from the porch swing onto my lap. She nuzzles against my chest and purrs with contentment.

"You call sitting a few feet from the front door of our cabin running off? Jagger, you are too much." Her words come out muffled as her mouth trails kisses along my neck.

The warm breath makes me shudder. I rumble deep in my chest as my hands roam over her lush curves. Covered by a maxi dress. I growl in frustration.

"And you're in clothes. Seclusion Rule number two you've broken. *Bad* mate!" I chide as I spank her ass cheek.

She yelps and wiggles on my lap, waking my cock for another round. And I'm all for it. One hundred percent!

Since we made love after our mate bonding ceremony, something about Sage has fueled a hunger in me I've never experienced before. I don't know if it's because she's all mine finally, we have the bullshit with our pack and coven behind us, or just being in love. Fuck if I know. But I'm not complaining in any way, shape, or form.

But today marks the last day of our seclusion. The pack will arrive soon for a night run to celebrate our bonding. It's a tradition I cannot deny them. I grumble just at the thought of having more than our enforcers, Ulf, and his mate—who cooks for us—around. Fortunately for the males, they've kept their distance knowing the protective instincts of an Alpha go off the charts when he takes his mate to seclusion.

And mine are even worse given the fact we had to fight so hard to stay together. Ten fucking years apart, then dealing with those still wanting to keep us separated. I was on the verge of an all-out war or walk away from all of it. Thank the Fates it's all settled on both sides.

"Does that mean you're going to punish me, my Alpha?"

My fated mate's question captures my attention. She wiggles her round ass on my lap. My cock gives her what she seeks as it thickens and lengthens along her hip. She purrs and presses kisses against my stumbled jaw. Her mouth leaves a scorching trail as it makes its way to cover mine.

I slant my mouth over hers for a dominating kiss. She moans as my tongue slides into her wet heat and sweeps around to taste every bit of her. On a mewl, she lifts her tongue to tangle with mine. I groan and shift to place her back on the swing and kneel between her spread thighs.

She stares up at me, panting for breath. I stare back as I hold the base of my cock and push the swing back. On the return, I impale her on my dick. Then repeat the move. As the swing arcs back and forth, my fated mate cries out in wild abandon. Her fingers grip the edge of the swing as her chest heaves. On a return, I lower my mouth to bite her plump brown nipple through the gauzy fabric of her maxi dress. She wails.

We continue our adult version of a day at the playground until I drag out multiple orgasms from her quivering pussy. She slumps back against the swing in a state of sheer euphoria. Her eyes hooded. Lips parted. Thighs twitching. I blew my mate's mind.

With a roar, I plunge into her soaking pussy once more and cum so hard *my* mind blanks. I slump over her and bury my face against the crook of her neck. My tongue darts out to lap at the sweat coating my claiming bite. The night of our mate bonding ceremony, I reenforced it with a fresh claim. Lest anyone not notice my first mark.

The distant sound of laughter filters through my carnal haze. I growl. The pack arrived. Damn!

"Now, baby, you'll stay here with Njal, the rest of your security detail, and some elders who chose not to shift for the pack run. The pack understands you haven't shifted yet. They still love their Luna, as do I."

A secret smile plays on my fated mate's gorgeous face. Her eyes shine as she stares up at me in the clearing outside of our cabin. The rest of the pack—some in human form, others as wolves—wait for my signal to bound off for our celebratory run. I squeeze her hip bones where my hands rest as I raise my eyebrow in question.

"What are you not telling me, Sage Larson Waters?" I ask using my Alpha command as leverage.

She gnaws on her bottom lip, eyes wide.

I squeeze again as she hesitates, and she yelps and hops onto her toes.

"O—okay… Okay! I can shift now."

My mouth drops open. What the hell? When did that happen? Better yet, how did I not notice?

She giggles, and I realize I spoke aloud, especially since the pack turns to stare at us. I ignore them and wait for Sage to answer me.

She places my hand on her lower belly. The shine in her emerald green eyes increases with unshed tears. I frown, concerned the dinner we ate earlier upset her stomach. But it was only grilled fish and vegetables. A light fare prior to the pack run. She passed on the Chardonnay—

"Jagger, the night of our mate bonding ceremony, I felt the spark indicating we conceived."

I stare at her blankly. What?

She shakes her head and speaks again.

"Jagger Waters Larson, I am pregnant with your pups!"

My eyes snap to her belly, where she cups my hand against it. I glance back up at my fated mate, and she nods.

"Twins, a male and a female. *Your pups,*" she whispers as the tears leak from her eyes.

I fall to my knees in front of my fated mate, the mother of my unborn pups. *My life!*

My forehead presses to her still flat belly. Now tears gather in *my* eyes as I murmur thanks to the Fates. Sage runs her fingers through my hair as my entire body shakes with emotion. I barely register the pack as they raise a song of joyful howls to the star-studded sky above.

I place two kisses on my fated mate's belly, one for each pup. Soon it will grow round with my heirs. At that moment, I know the foretold prophecy will come to pass, and I will allow no one to stand in the way of my pups' futures. No. One.

EPILOGUE

he Everglades

THE RAVEN GLIDES on the air currents. Its glossy ebony wings spread wide as it circles above the tops of the pine trees. Its obsidian eyes flick across the wetlands below. The raven sees every movement as the female and male stand amongst the others. Just as it had for the past seven days and six nights. It never strayed far from the pair.

Yet, they never noted it flying above or sitting on a branch, even on the windowsill of their cabin.

The raven makes certain to blend in as best it can despite being larger than the average raven and the closet population is in Georgia, miles away from the Everglades.

But the female and male pay no heed as they fornicate like feral beasts all day and all night long.

The raven's body shudders at the memories, feathers flutter.

It takes a last turn over those below, then settles on a tree branch high above them. Although close enough to hear their every word.

"Jagger Waters Larson, I am pregnant with your pups!" The female declares.

The male's eyes snap to her flat belly, where she cups his hand against it lovingly. Dumbfounded, the male glances back up at the female, who nods.

"Twins, a male and a female. *Your pups.*"

Even though it's a whisper, the raven hears it as though the female spoke to its face.

A croaking sound rips past its ebony beak. The raven almost falls from its hidden perch.

A few of those gathered turn in its direction. Their sharp eyesight detects the raven amongst the boughs of the pine tree. Heads cock curious as to the reason the raven would utter such a devastated cry.

Before they can approach, the raven leaps from its perch, ebony wings spread out, and it flaps hard to reach the star-filled sky above. Satisfied it's far enough from those below, the raven circles the female and the male once more.

With a parting strangled croak, it banks towards the north.

∼

THANK you for reading *Jagger The Temptation: A Wolf Shifter Fated Mates Paranormal Romance*!

If you enjoyed the book, I would so appreciate your review as they make a huge difference for indie authors. Be sure to sign up for my newsletter for the latest info about the series, new releases, and a FREE book at **bit.ly/ CLBooksDylanTheRogue!** Next up: *Rust The Rejected: A Wolf Shifter Rejected Mate Paranormal Romance.* Turn the page for a preview.

PREVIEW RUST THE REJECTED: A WOLF SHIFTER REJECTED MATE PARANORMAL ROMANCE

ust

"OH, my, Dr. Ingolf. What a big stethoscope you have, Sir. So long and hard. Ooo and look! It even has a shiny tip. Shall I blow on it to warm it for you, Sir?"

The submissive purses her full glossy lips as she stares up at me from the velvet pillow between my feet. A rich chocolate brown rims her dilated pupils.

But it's the sight of her pillowy tits overflowing the cups of her pink lace corset that makes my cock leak pre-cum. The perfect size to fit in my large hands and soft. Nothing against silicone enhancements, but the feel of naturally lush tits with pinchable plump nipples wins.

My mouth salivates as much as my cock drips.

The Alpha Dom in me knows I should correct the

sub's forward behavior. I did not command her to fist my dick—only to kneel. Any other time, I would toss her over my thighs and spank her round ass. The globes on either side of the skimpy lace thong would match its color for a delightful rosy shade. My palm itches for the punishment.

Instead, I sigh and pinch the bridge of my nose—not a nipple.

I've had back-to-back nights as a critical care surgeon at Miami's busiest hospital emergency room. The urban location has more than its share of acute, life-threatening injuries that require immediate surgery. Trained to perform well under pressure, I never hesitate to pick up the scalpel to save a patient.

My duties require the utmost focus. I cannot allow distractions. A patient's life—many times their heart—is in my hands, literally.

So, when I have a rare night off from the ER and no one in our pack needs Dr. Ingolf, I don't waste it. I take advantage of the opportunity to revel in my dominate proclivities.

A trip to Club Sol & Mani Miami provides a safe space for those in the BDSM lifestyle. The luxury, members-only club on Ocean Drive owned by the Miami Wolves Pack promises a night of pleasure.

I let my gaze return to the sub. She winks at me. Uh. No.

"Oh, naughty pet, how you misbehave," I tsk as I tuck my cock back into my bespoke trousers and zip up. Her mouth droops in dismay. "I must let the resident Dom know you like to top from the bottom."

Her glossy lips pout as elegantly shaped eyebrows pinch together and mar her pretty face. The little she-wolf even dares to growl at my reprimand.

Well, damn. That will never do.

She yelps as I scoop her from the pillow and over my muscular thighs. Long blonde hair falls over her face like a silky curtain. Her hands scrabble for the floor while her shapely legs flail.

I trap them with one of mine and press a hand between her shoulder blades to still her movements. A deep growl of my own halts her wiggling. Then a swat to her left ass cheek makes her jolt.

"Enough with this, naughty pet. You will take your punishment like a well-trained Club Sol & Mani sub. Twenty spanks, and you will count each one. Miss one, and we start anew. Do you understand?"

She shivers as I add Alpha power to my words. The musky scent of her arousal flares. I inhale deeply. My cock throbs, and my wolf howls. Yeah, it's been a while.

"Yes, Sir. I apologize and will behave appropriately."

I smirk as my palm rubs the soft skin of her upturned ass. A moan slips past her lips, and her pelvis tilts to push her ass into my hand.

THWACK.

"You disobey during a punishment?"

Her ass lowers as she shakes her head. Blonde strands sway with the light catching the golden streaks.

"Words, naughty pet. I will have your words."

"N—No, Sir."

"Count, or we start from one."

"One, Sir." She replies immediately.

Halfway through, the intoxicating scent of her arousal permeates the air in my private suite. A damp patch of it spreads through the wool of my trousers. I rim her slick pussy lips with the calloused tip of my middle finger.

She gasps, and her greedy core clenches. Then she wails when I issue three successive spanks to her swollen folds. But she doesn't miss the count.

I thrust two tapered fingers inside of her pussy. It pulsates around the digits, sucking them in deep. So tight and wet. I stifle a groan. Too damn long.

"Twenty, Sir."

The sub ends on a choked pant.

I lift her to straddle my lap.

Tears stream down her reddened cheeks. Like her ass, they bear a crimson shade. I pull the Ferragamo silk pocket square from my suit jacket and dab her face. Chocolate brown eyes now softened lower to stare at my chest submissively.

"You did well, pet. Now, you will think twice before topping a Dom. Won't you?" I ask with a cocked eyebrow.

"Thank you, Sir. Yes, I will," she whispers.

"Good. Now, we fuck," I say as my hands cup her heated ass, and I rise. Quick strides take me to the sex swing. Even quicker, I strap her in.

Excitement shines in her eyes, even as she keeps them

lowered. Her teeth nibble at the corner of her mouth. Dainty fingers wrap around the black suede straps. Her thighs—slick with her juices—quiver in anticipation.

She doesn't have long to wait.

I unzip my trousers, and my aching cock springs free. It slaps back against my shirt. The engorged mushroom tip reaches my belly button. I slip a condom over it.

Teeth marks dimple her lip as she moans at the sight of my dick.

I fist its wide base and stroke up the veiny shaft once, squeezing below the head. Pearly beads of pre-cum drip to floor. Her lust-filled eyes follow their descent. Then snap to my face when I grab her hips and pull.

The sex swing arcs forward. We watch as her pussy swallows the length and girth of my cock. The tip parts her glistening folds, then disappears inch by delicious inch into her soaked core. When my heavy balls meet her heated ass cheeks, we groan in unison.

My eyes close. The sensation of tight, wet warmth clamping on my dick makes my balls tingle. Finally. Fuuuck. I relish the moment before I withdraw to my tip.

The sub mewls in protest at the loss.

"Oh, little pet, I will satisfy you many times over. But you will not cum until I give you permission. Do you understand?"

"Yes, Sir, thank you, Sir!"

I chuckle wickedly and pull the sex swing forward to plunge back in. With each arc of the swing, her pussy flutters around my cock. Too much and I draw back, edging her until she begs to cum.

The forceful thrusts pop her tits from the corset. I lean over and suckle the plump nipples. She moans as her inner walls clench around my cock. A few more thrusts, and my control hangs on by a thread.

"Now, pet! Keep cumming until I give you permission to stop," I growl.

She keens as her first orgasm causes her body to buck in the sex swing.

I grunt and growl as I fuck her through one wave after the other of her toe-curling orgasms until she's limp in the swing. Then I chase my release with a roar to the ceiling. My knees turn to jelly, and my still erect cock slips from her pussy.

She whimpers.

I tuck my junk away, then uncuff her from the sex swing and carry her to the bed. With a sated sigh, she rolls to her side, curled up like a well-fed pup. I chuckle to myself as head to the en suite bathroom for a warm, moistened cloth and clean her gently. I apply a soothing salve to her warm crimson ass cheeks, and she moans softly. Tucked beneath the silk sheets, I leave the contented she-wolf with a note beside her pillow to stay the night and enjoy breakfast.

I skip the shower and go downstairs to my McLaren P1 LM. The ride to my bayfront mansion on our pack's Moon Island in Biscayne Bay brings me back to reality.

I let my mind wander as I drive along Collins Avenue,

South Beach in my rearview mirror. And as my thoughts have in recent months, they go to what I long for to complete my life. No matter how successful I am in the ER or how many—or how few—nights at Club Sol & Mani, one thing still eludes me.

My fated mate…

Click the Image Below or Visit books2read.com/u/ baonL6 For Your Copy

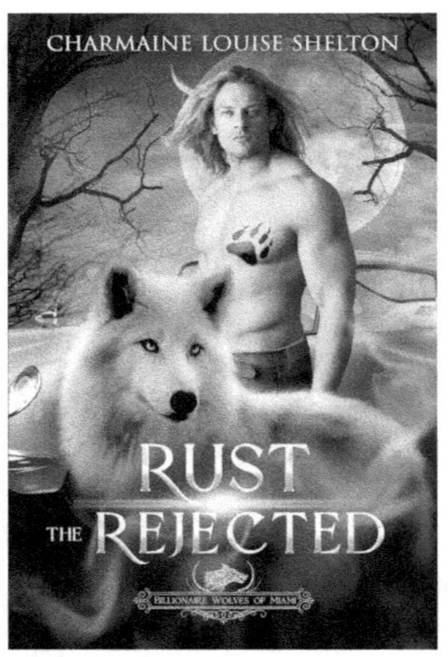

**Rust The Rejected: A Wolf Shifter Rejected Mate
Paranormal Romance**

WANT FREE BOOKS?

Want to know what happened to Jagger's best friend Dylan? Find out in *Dylan The Rogue: A Wolf Shifter Fated Mates Paranormal Romance* your FREE Book!

Click Cover Below or visit **bit.ly/ CLBooksDylanTheRogue** to subscribe to my newsletter for latest news and launches, books from my author friends, and sizzling reads in book promotions. Plus, start reading the steamy fated mates romance for bad boy wolf shifter Dylan.

WANT FREE BOOKS?

FREE BOOK!

NEVER RELEASED!

EXCLUSIVE FOR SUBSCRIBERS!

ALSO BY CHARMAINE LOUISE SHELTON

STEELE INTERNATIONAL, INC.
A BILLIONAIRES ROMANCE SERIES
Discover My Desires Sebastian & Lola Prequel
(Available Exclusively to Subscribers)

Fulfill My Desires Sebastian & Lola Part I

Heighten My Desires Sebastian & Lola Part II

Ignite My Desires Roger & Leonie Part I

Stoke My Desires Roger & Leonie Part II

Justify My Desires Roger & Leonie Part III

Deepen My Desires Sebastian & Lola Part III

Capture My Desires Malcolm & Starr Part I

Embrace My Desires Malcolm & Starr Part II

Cherish My Desires Malcolm & Starr Part III

A Trilogy of Desires Sebastian & Lola Parts I-III

A Trilogy of Desires Roger & Leonie Parts I-III

Series Extras

Series Playlist

STEELE INTERNATIONAL, INC. - JACKSON CORPORATION
A BILLIONAIRES ROMANCE SERIES CROSSOVER
Tempt My Desires Lachlan & Haley Part I

Tease My Desires Lachlan & Haley Part I

Grant My Desires Lachlan & Haley Part III

JACKSON CORPORATION
A BILLIONAIRES ROMANCE SERIES
Evoke My Desires Laurent & Yessenia Prequel

Light My Desires Laurent & Yessenia Part I

BILLIONAIRE WOLVES SERIES
WOLF SHIFTER FATED MATES PARANORMAL ROMANCE

MIAMI
Jagger The Awakening
(Available Exclusively for a Limited Time in Lunar Rising: A Collection of Paranormal Romance)

Dylan The Rogue
(Available Exclusively to Subscribers)

Jagger The Temptation

Rust The Rejected

ABOUT CHARMAINE LOUISE SHELTON

Charmaine Louise Shelton loves a dominant Alpha hero—human, shifter, or vampire—as long as he's a billionaire and sexy as sin! Her romance novels take readers into the heroes' glitzy, glamorous, steamy worlds as they chase after independent women who unexpectedly capture their hearts. Want to experience some more? Download a free book at CharmaineLouiseBooks.com!

Find her at:
CharmaineLouiseBooks.com

Follow her on social media on your favorite channels below and **download your Free Book** at CharmaineLouise Books.com.

Fulfill Your Desires.

DEDICATION

To my awesome and dedicated beta readers and ARC Team, my amazing author friends, and this incredible community for their support.

And most of all to you, my loyal readers who love these couples as much as I do.

Thank you!

Cover Design: Murphy Wallace, Midnight Designs

Fulfill Your Desires.

xoxo
Charmaine Louise Shelton

www.ingramcontent.com/pod-product-compliance
Lightning Source LLC
Chambersburg PA
CBHW070456200726
48293CB00007B/2241